WICKEDEST WITCH

PARANORMAL ROMANTIC COMEDY

EVE LANGLAIS

SECOND EDITION

Copyright © 2013, Eve Langlais

Cover Art @ 2023 Addictive Covers

Produced in Canada

Published by Eve Langlais

http://www.EveLanglais.com

ALL RIGHTS RESERVED

Wickedest Witch is a work of fiction and the characters, events and dialogue found within the story are of the author's imagination and are not to be construed as real. Any resemblance to actual events or persons, either living or deceased, is completely coincidental.

No part of this book may be reproduced or shared in any form or by any means, electronic or mechanical, including but not limited to digital copying, file sharing, audio recording, email and printing without permission in writing from the author.

E-ISBN: 978-1-927459-38-6

KDP ISBN: 9781484980668

Ingram: 978-1-77384-006-2

PROLOGUE

"I don't think we should see each other anymore," said her boyfriend of three months, practically a record for her.

The nerve of him. Breaking up with her, and in person. Evangeline would have never thought he had the balls to do it face to face. She'd always pictured Derek more as an email or texting kind of guy.

"May I ask why?" She didn't really care; however, she couldn't deny a curiosity as to his reason. Her last few boyfriends just stopped calling and moved without leaving a forwarding address. Despite the brevity of their relationships, they'd known her well enough to not stick around.

"You're just too evil for me," Derek answered with a shrug, ducking his head in an attempt to appear apologetic.

Too evil? Most women would have taken offense at his claim, but he spoke the truth, a nasty habit of his. What a shock, though, that he acted as if it were a flaw. Could she help her natural inclination to do harm instead of good? So she possessed malevolent tendencies, it wasn't as if she killed people—often. *The way I look at it is if they're too mentally deficient to get out of my way then they deserve to die before they do something even more dim-witted, such as procreate.* Evangeline held a low tolerance for people she deemed TSTL – too stupid to live. *Congratulations, Derek, you've just become the newest member of that group.*

What made the remark by her ex-lover ironic was Derek made his living as a thief, but unlike Robin Hood, he didn't steal to give to the poor. Derek stole to supplement his extravagant lifestyle, yet the smug bastard had the *nerve* to call her evil? Not to mention, break up with her? *I decide when things are over. Not this pathetic excuse for a man.*

"Is there any particular reason you chose to break up with me now?" So close to her sister's wedding and totally messing up her plans to bring a plus one. "It's not like you didn't know my reputation before we began seeing each other," she commented, pursing her lips and placing her hands on her hips, a sign of agitation he foolishly ignored.

Derek ran a hand through his thinning hair. "I heard the rumors, but I thought they were exaggerated. I didn't think you were that bad. I mean, come on. Did you really have to turn all their candy into broccoli? They were just kids and you made them cry."

Evangeline wanted to roll her eyes. *I can't believe he's still harping on that. It happened weeks ago.* "I don't approve of Halloween, making fun of witches and what not," she said. She couldn't help her yearly annoyance at the way the media had bastardized a sacred holiday, one the mystical society she belong to revered. "Served them right. Besides, isn't the media always telling us that children need to eat healthier?" The parents of those brats should have thanked her for saving their progeny from obesity.

"See? This is why I can't be with you. You just don't get it."

"Get what?" She frowned.

"Anything. You're a cold-hearted witch, Evangeline, which is why I think it's best if we stop seeing each other."

"I don't believe this. You're dumping me." It still blew her away that he dared to. It also occurred to her she should feel something, anything; after all, they'd dated—make that screwed—for close to three months, a new record for her. Yet, as she looked upon his lanky frame, she didn't feel any remorse or anguish. No urge to throw herself at him sobbing for him to change his mind. Nope. Nothing so weak and girly. On the other hand, annoyance bubbled and her pride kicked in.

How dare he break up with me, and right before my sister's wedding too. Now where would she find a date—she'd scared off most of the male population already. As for those that remained, well, they were single for a reason.

"I'm sure you'll find someone else. Someone who will..." He paused for a moment as he searched for a diplomatic end to his sentence. She should have told him not to bother. "Appreciate your unique qualities."

"Derek, you really aren't too bright, are you? Then again, I didn't date you for your brains." No, she'd dated him for the sex—Derek lacked many things, but he sported a thick one and, with a little direction from her, learned how to use it. Evangeline arched a perfect brow at him and smiled sweetly, perhaps a tad too much judging by his blanching face. "You really should have ignored Ms. Manners and done this from a much safer location—say on another continent. Goodbye, Derek." With a waggle of her fingers, Evangeline drew on her innate magical power. She never tired of the rush as the energy of the ether filled her and tingled inside.

Poor Derek, too late he realized his mistake. He backed away, hands held up in a pleading gesture. Her grin stretched wider as he turned and prepared to run. As if he could escape her wrath.

Thrusting out her hand, she focused the power within her, concentrating and shaping it to her will. She flung the result at his fleeing back. It struck him dead center and spread until it encased him from head to toe in a brilliant white light. When the glow dissipated, a puddle of clothes littered the ground and amongst them sat a large rat.

Bringing her fingers to her lips, she blew on them, gunslinger style. She enjoyed meting out karma, or in this case, giving a dirty rat a body to match his actions.

With a squeak, Derek scurried off and Evangeline laughed. To think he'd had the nerve to break up with her. He should count himself lucky she hadn't turned him into a grease spot.

They didn't call *her* the Wickedest Witch for nothing.

1

SLOUCHED ON A BAR STOOL, RYKER PERUSED THE PATRONS around him. A soothing drunken buzz muted the natters of the crowd and made the buck-toothed shifter—*by the smell, I'd say rabbit*—beside him appear more attractive than he recalled when he first arrived. And people said alcohol didn't make things better. In this case, it turned a homely jack rabbit into someone he could fuck. Oh who was he kidding? He didn't really care what she looked like. *I'm horny and any female body will do.*

Lurching toward her, he tripped over his own feet and staggered hard against the bar. Startled, his intended prey scurried off.

"Damn." Stymied and with no other prospects nearby, Ryker perched back on his stool and signaled Barry behind the bar for another beer.

Barry shook his bald head at him. "I think you've had quite enough, old friend. Time you called it a night."

"What are you? My mutha?" slurred Ryker. *Okay, so I might be a little drunk. Big fucking deal. I'm a big boy, and it's not as if I'm driving.* Like a certain movie pirate, he'd stagger, stagger, and if needed, crawl his way home. Or sleep in a gutter until the drunkenness wore off. He'd travelled this road before.

"What's up with you?" asked Barry as he wiped down the bar in front of him. "I've never seen you like this. Does this have anything to do with your visit back home?"

Yes! "Nope." As if he'd orate aloud the details of that embarrassment. So much for doing his family proud and following tradition. Before someone took him for a big family guy, it should be noted Ryker didn't give a flying fuck about maintaining the purity of the family genes, or strengthening their position in the pack. Nope. Not him. He left those kinds of politics and shit to his other brothers usually. Usually being the key word. So why had he returned to the bosom of his pack when summoned? Why had he agreed to the farce his parents had their hearts set on, mainly marriage to a stranger? He'd done it – like some pansy, apron-tied wuss — for his mother.

Gawd, just thinking about it made him want to hack up a hairball or hit something until it begged for mercy, but he'd settle for another drink, if Barry would just shut the fuck up and give him one. He slapped a fiver on the bar.

Ignoring it, Barry kept drying the glass in his hands. "Want to talk about it?"

"Nope." Hell, he'd scrub it with sandpaper from his brain if he could. He slid the money closer.

Barry nudged it back. They engaged in a see-saw that involved the tattered bill for a few moments before Barry fixed him with a hard look. Ryker gave him his best pathetic look. Yeah, it didn't work on his mother, and it sure didn't work on his friend.

Barry shook his head and sighed. "Dude, drinking won't make whatever happened go away."

"Dass what you tink," replied Ryker. With a shake of his head, he tried to dislodge the cloud that fogged his mind and words. It just made the bloody room spin more erratically. Barry really should talk to an engineer about the problem. Right after he got Ryker a beer. It took him a blink, okay, two, before he realized Barry had wandered off to serve other folks.

Traitor. Just for that, I should take my business elsewhere. He knew a fridge with a cold six-pack that wouldn't give him attitude. But, going home alone didn't appeal. He leaned his chin on the bar and stared in the mirror to see if there was anyone left with an X-chromosome drunk enough to take him on. The remaining pickings in the bar had devolved into single, hopeful men like himself and a few couples. Preferring pussy, that knocked the guys out, and as for the duos, Ryker did not do threesomes, well, except that one time with the best friends—there wasn't a man alive who would have said no to that pair of wood nymphs. What a night that turned out to be. Pity they'd never called back. Then again, maybe he should thank his lucky stars. Last he heard, they'd gone to the forest to root and raise saplings. Not his, thank God. How he would have explained to his mother that she had trees for grandchildren he didn't know.

With no single lady in sight, and no beer forthcoming, Ryker decided it was time to leave. Standing proved a tad more difficult than expected, though, especially when the room began to tilt and spin, much like the ride at the amusement park his niece made him go on. Sitting down hard, Ryker rested his arms on the counter and put his face in his hands.

This is fucking pathetic. How far he'd fallen. Letting family and a woman—a woman he didn't even love or like—sink him so low.

The bitter scent of coffee—black and strong enough to sprout hair on even the smoothest of chests—drifted into his cocoon of self-inflicted misery.

"Drink up, old man," said his best friend, make that only friend, Barry. An acerbic tongue and hot temper did not endear Ryker to many people.

Wrapping big hands around the warm mug, Ryker gulped down some of the piping hot brew, the instant caffeine jolt bringing some clarity back to his mind. "Thanks," he mumbled.

"Anytime. And when you're ready to tell me what happened, give me a shout. You know I'll listen. You're not the only one who's had to deal with pack shit." Poor Barry. As a grizzly bear who hated living in the woods, he'd gone through his own version of hell when he decided to leave the mountains for the city. To this day, his family still refused to speak to him.

"I know." And eventually, he would unburden himself. Probably even do a little jig he didn't get roped into a marriage he'd neither searched for nor wanted. But right now, with the humiliation fresh, he wanted to marinate in his misery a while longer.

With each sip of the coffee, the spinning and haze in his head got better, the bitter brew and his metabolism working to clear the alcohol from his system. As he drained the last of the java and put the cup down, the door to the bar opened, and in blew a sharp, cold breeze. It also brought with it a stranger bearing a tantalizing scent. A woman whom Ryker noticed immediately, as did his inner beast. It woke with a rumble and urged him to take a closer sniff.

Why? His inner feline didn't reply. Unlike what some people thought, those who could shift in to beasts couldn't actually speak to their inner creatures. All their interaction occurred with feelings, primitive, base emotions and urges. It didn't mean Ryker didn't understand what his cat wanted. That was more than clear. It wanted him to go sniff the female's butt. Shove his nose right between her thighs and inhale deep.

Drunk or not, Ryker suspected that wouldn't go over well. His uncle Fred had spent time in jail for doing that one too many times.

Explaining legalities to his cat, though, didn't quite work. His feline insisted they investigate. He tossed another why his kitty's way. Pacing the edges of his mind, the only thing his feline could convey was yummy.

Gonna have to give me a better reason than because she smells good. Because, personally, Ryker found the broad a tad too skinny for his taste. Then again, given she was the only woman in the place...*I guess beggars can't be choosers.* On the plus side, though, she didn't need a paper bag over her head.

Model slim and tall, her long, straight black hair framed an angular face. Perfectly arched brows accented her sharp brown gaze while her lips, painted a bright red, thinned into a straight line. Seemed he wasn't the only one less than impressed with the view. He watched as she debated with herself; stay or go. Only because of his close scrutiny did he notice the moment she made her decision; her shoulders slumped a fraction, only for a brief moment, before squaring. Head held high, she sauntered to the bar as if she owned the place and ordered a glass of red wine.

A woman with attitude. Nice.

The sweet smell of shampoo and a musky perfume wafted over from her direction and Ryker's nose twitched —along with a body part further south. As if bespelled— despite the impossibility—Ryker found himself unable to look away. *I have to talk to her.*

As if feeling his stare upon her, the woman glanced over, cool and appraising. Raising a brow, she looked him up and down before meeting his gaze with a condescending smirk on her bright red lips. Some guys would have found it a turn off, not him. Just ask his swelling cock—women with character always drew him.

His mouth curled into a masculine grin that had gotten more than one pair of panties dropped. He clearly heard her snort and caught her disdainful sniff before she turned away, dismissing him.

Ryker's dark brows drew together in consternation. What the fuck? No woman came into a bar this time of night alone unless she was looking for a hook up. Even drunk, most women fawned over him, or at least the ones with a bit of back bone. The timid types tended to find his size a tad intimidating. So what was her deal? Did she bat for the other team? What a waste of pussy.

Barry, seeing his scowl, came over with a chuckle. "Don't feel bad, Ryker. She's a cold one."

"You know her?" Ryker asked, still facing her even though she'd given him her ramrod straight back.

Lowering his voice, Barry leaned closer. "I know who she is, and I can say with great confidence that you'd have to be insane to get involved with her even for one night."

"Why?" The warning intrigued him.

"You are looking at the Wickedest Witch."

"Not *the Wickedest Witch*."

"The one and only."

Well, hot damn. The name, an infamous one whispered about almost as much as his, caught Ryker's attention and he swiveled toward Barry. "Are you sure?"

"Oh it's her all right. She started coming to the bar around the time you left for home."

Ryker shook his head. "No way. You're fucking with me. I thought she was supposed to be an old crone." He'd definitely pictured her more haglike. Warty even.

"She could be," whispered Barry while shooting nervous glances at the woman. "She is a witch after all. I've heard they can cast spells to make themselves look like anyone they want."

If that were true, then what a shame she'd chosen tall and skinny because Ryker preferred his women with a little plush; it made the pumping more comfortable. However, beggars couldn't be choosers, and Ryker still had an itch. "Spell or not, I'm horny. As for her reputation, I know from experience how exaggerated those are. I mean, look at her. She seems harmless."

"For now."

"Come on, how bad could she be?" And really, what could she do to hurt him? He outweighed her by probably at least eighty pounds. If he couldn't handle a skinny witch, then he needed a neutering and a frilly dress.

Barry laughed, a sound he quickly tempered. "Appearances can be deceiving. Trust me when I say she is just as bad as the rumors indicate. You remember Derek?"

Vaguely—a punk ass thief with some magical skill for cloaking. "What about him?"

"He dated her for a while, and then one day, he disappeared. Sources say she turned him into a door mat. Or was that a dormouse. I don't quite recall other than it wasn't really nice."

Ryker put little stock in rumors, especially since there were plenty flying around about him, and while some held a semblance of truth, others would rival the tallest tales. *Witch or not, I want to get to know her. Something about her is pulling at me.* Not to mention his beast hadn't stopped pacing and chuffing inside since it had scented her. Besides, he liked a challenge. To boldly go where no man dared.

"Derek's a wimp," said Ryker. "A pretty girl like her needs a man—a real man."

"And let me guess, you think you're that guy?" said Barry, rolling his eyes. "Care to wager on it?"

"Damned straight. What are we playing for?" Ryker found himself perking up from the funk he'd languished in since his return to town.

"I wager you can't even get her to smile."

A chuckle escaped him. Way too easy. Ryker grinned. "You're on."

"What are we playing for?"

"I win and you let me drink free for the next week."

"Lose and you tell me what happened when you went home."

Cocky and confident, Ryker didn't hesitate slapping

his hand against Barry's. "You're on. Better prepare to call your beer suppliers. I feel a week long binge coming on."

Barry snorted as Ryker strutted his stuff over to the witch.

Piece of fucking cake.

2

THE BIG BRUTE, WHO'D EYED HER SINCE THE MOMENT SHE walked in, lurched over to the stool alongside her and Evangeline restrained a shudder at the alcoholic stench he emitted. Had he *bathed* in the beer? Her nose wrinkled in distaste as she tried to ignore his imposing presence, not an easy task.

Built on the lines of a brick house, the man took up a lot of space, and most of it appeared as muscle, not fat. A point in his favor given she disliked overweight slobs. The stranger might have achieved passably attractive had he at least shaven the bristly shadow that covered his face and run a comb through his shaggy mop of dark hair. Intoxicated, and dressed one step above a vagrant—IE stained plaid shirt buttoned incorrectly with grease-stained, well-worn jeans—he redefined the term diamond in the rough.

The interest in his bloodshot eyes made her want to sigh. *Great. I wonder what lame pickup line he's going to try.* If this weren't the closest magic friendly bar in town, she'd have stopped popping in for a drink after completing her most recent job, but sometimes, a witch wanted to relax in the company of other people—make that beings—without trying to hide behind a mask of humanity. Not to mention she still hadn't found an escort for her sister's wedding and with the date drawing closer, just about any man, or creature, would do. Or not, she thought as she caught a whiff of her new neighbor.

"Hey there, cutie. I don't suppose you'd give me a smile?" Her would-be suitor grinned at her engagingly, and while another type of woman might have found it endearing, Evangeline had yet to move on from her men-were-scum stage. Derek's break up with her still rankled. Too evil indeed. Just the reminder heightened her already foul mood, which was why it surprised her to realize that something about him made her libido take notice. With a yawn and a stretch, her body woke and urged her to say hello, and not just with her mouth. Something about the stranger apparently appealed, which totally pissed her off. She hated not controlling every aspect of her life and body.

"Why don't you try your lame pickup line on someone a little drunker and blonder?" She gave him credit when his smile didn't falter.

"Lucky me, you're not just cute, you come with a shit-load of attitude. Have I mentioned I like that in a woman?"

"I'd prefer you not speak to me at all."

"And leave a gorgeous babe like yourself to drink all alone? Doesn't seem right if you ask me."

Gorgeous? She snorted. He only saw what she wanted

him to see. What she showed the world. "No one's asking you, and I didn't come here to get hit on."

"Plans change."

"So do the seasons. So why don't you make like a bird and migrate somewhere else?"

The idiot laughed and damn him if the rumble didn't strike a chord and thaw a spot inside. "Lady, I am liking you more and more."

"The feeling is not mutual."

Despite her attempts to give him the brush off, he proved tenacious. "Come on, you know you think I'm hot. What say you and I head over to my place and get to know each other in a more intimate sense? The springs in my mattress could use some exercise." He didn't just say it, he waggled his brows at her suggestively.

The unmitigated gall of him. Evangeline's eyes widened at his crude attempt to get in her panties, then she scowled as said panties turned damp, her body not minding his temerity one bit. "I'm going to pretend you didn't just say that. Now leave before I turn you into a toad." Her unexpected bodily reaction made her tone and words harsh. She didn't like the baffling erotic interest her body had for this stranger. *Has he cast a lust spell on me?* Or was she that starved for male attention that any thug with a cock between his legs would do?

"A toad? Don't they have long tongues? A girl who likes her oral. Lucky you, I love to give and receive."

"That wasn't meant to be an invitation," she snapped.

"Really? Because it sounded like foreplay to me. Tell you what, how about instead of you making me into a frog, I turn into your bucking bronco and you can be the cowgirl that likes to ride astride." He said this with a cocky grin, a thrust of his hips, and finished with a wink.

Her jaw dropped at his effrontery, then tightened. She could hear the barkeep's guffaws as he unabashedly listened in. *The nerve! I'll teach him to fuck with a witch.* She ignored the titillating vision he painted even as her body reacted, her nipples tightening in interest.

Drawing on her inner power, and coiling it for use, Evangeline waggled her fingers and...nothing happened. Frowning, she wiggled them again and pushed harder at her magic, aiming it right at his impossible to miss bull's-eye of a chest. Again, nada.

The drunken idiot laughed. "Sorry, little witch. I'm protected against direct magic, being a shifter and all, but I promise I can still make lots of magic happen in the bedroom."

Figured the idiot with the crass pickup lines would be a bloody shifter and immune to her spells. Darned nuisances. Where was animal control when you needed them? Then again, why have someone else handle the problem when she was more than capable? Evangeline had more than one trick up her sleeve. Hooking her foot around the bottom of the stool he perched on, she yanked it and dumped her would-be suitor on the floor. She also poured her glass of wine over him for good measure.

As he lay there looking dumbfounded, she laughed aloud, her voice husky with derision. "Consider that a no," she said with a cold smile before sidestepping his prone body and heading for the door. She swept out into the night, puzzled at the fact her pulse raced and her cheeks were flushed with heat. Good thing her glamour hid the signs. She'd hate for word to get around that an animal managed to fluster her. Now if only she could figure out how he'd done it.

How did that uncouth beast turn me on? Even stranger, why does a part of me wish I'd accepted his offer and gone back to his place to check out the springs in his mattress?

3

RYKER ROSE FROM THE BAR FLOOR AND SHOOK HIMSELF—like a wet dog, wine drops flying—before sitting back on his stool. Taking the towel Barry handed him, he rubbed at his damp hair, still in awe she'd dared to not only put him on his ass, but then dumped her drink on him to boot.

Fuck me, that woman has spunk. Betcha she'd be wild in bed. But could she handle a man like him? Those bony hips of hers could cause some serious bruises. *Maybe if I took her from behind, I could minimize the damage. Then again, I'd first have to convince her to spread her legs far enough to enjoy herself.* Somehow, he didn't think she'd part those thighs too quickly or easily.

The challenge intrigued him. Shot down or not, he couldn't help oddly lusting after her. He didn't come across too many women with her kind of balls.

Barry clucked his tongue in reprimand. "You just had to antagonize her, didn't you? Count yourself lucky you are a shifter, or right now I'd probably be mopping up a puddle."

"You're exaggerating. I bet you she's a pussy cat underneath all that attitude.

"A pussy cat?" His friend almost choked. "More like a deadly cougar with sharp claws."

"Lucky for her I've got a broad back for scratching and super healing powers. I wonder what it takes to get her to purr," Ryker mused.

"You do realize you're insane. Only a madman would risk his life trying to get close enough to try."

A madman or a curious cat. "All women have a soft spot. You just need to find it and stroke it just right." With a tongue or dick. "Now, given I made her laugh and smile—"

"Because she dumped your sorry ass on the ground."

"The how it occurred isn't the point. I got her to do it, which means I won, so hand over another beer, bartender, and tell me more about this wicked witch."

Ryker found his interest aroused—along with other parts—by her feisty attitude. The deadly tone she'd used when she threatened him had sent shivers—of a good kind—up and down Ryker's spine. Skinny or not, the female possessed courage, something Ryker rarely saw in women as they tended to find his size and reputation intimidating. *Even though I'd never hit a girl.* But not all women gave him a chance to prove he was a good guy at heart. Some took one look at him and assumed the worst. A prime example? His ex-fiancée. Was it any wonder he drank himself stupid after the way she humiliated him in front of family and friends?

He might only admit it to himself, but what a major

turn on it was to meet someone with the courage to stand up to him. What a pity, though, that the only available woman he'd found so far with that quality ended up a witch. *But damn, I bet she's wicked in bed.*

Barry handed him a frosty bottle of Coors Light, as in light on the alcohol. Ryker shot him a dirty look, which his friend ignored. Rubbing his chin, Barry mused aloud, "What do I know about the wickedest witch? Not much."

"It's probably more than me. All I know is people say her name like she's the kiss of death."

"She is—if you cross her. Again, so rumor says. You do know who her granddaddy is, right?"

"Um, no. Should I?"

"Rasputin."

"Who?"

"Rasputin as in the Russian sorcerer who had the czar dancing to his tune like a puppet on strings until the attempted assassination. History has it they poisoned him and when that didn't work, beat him, shot him four times, and then drowned him."

"And he survived?"

Barry's head bobbed up and down. "Although, they thought he was dead when they fished him from the water. They buried him, then dug him up and set him on fire. And then shit got weird."

"Weirder than their overzealous attempts to murder the man?"

"Apparently, he sat up, covered in flames, and walked away."

"No fucking way."

"Hey, I'm just telling it like it is. After that, though, Rasputin stayed away from politics. Some claim it's on account his daughter chained him in a dungeon because he turned into a brain-eating zombie."

"We had to do that to a great uncle of mine. He wouldn't put his human skin back on after his wife died and started going after humans."

"The point I was trying to make is she comes from some seriously evil stock."

Ryker snorted. "We all have family members we'd prefer to disown." Ryker knew all about the family black sheep, or in his case, panther. Whatever you wanted to call him, his pack would prefer he made himself scarce. "What else do you know? She's single, you were saying."

"As far as I know, and self-employed. She's got her own company. Wicked Incorporated."

"What does she do?"

"Odd jobs. Specialty jobs. Kind of like you, as a matter of fact. She's talent for hire. If you have a problem, be it a protection detail, surveillance, location of an artifact or person, she'll do it, for a steep price."

"Is she any good?"

"From what I hear? The best. Although, her methods aren't always the nicest. She tends to have a heavy hand when it comes to questioning people. Or should I say she's keen on threats and easy with the magic."

"Threats are an effective way of getting information. Nothing wrong with bending a few laws, breaking a few fingers, and dangling someone off a high balcony to get them to spill the beans."

A sound escaped Barry, a cross between a choke and a laugh. "Fuck me, I should have known you'd be the last person to think her tactics were too rough."

"Are you calling me a thug?"

"If the brass knuckles fit."

"Who needs those when a bare fist will do?" Ryker grinned and held up his weapon of choice before thumping it on the bar.

"You are such an idiot."

"And you need to dump out this piss you call a beer and hand me a bottle of the real stuff."

"You know, you're really making me wish she could have turned you in a frog just so I could have thrown you in that radioactive pond and watched you run from those mutant flies," Barry muttered as he handed over a frosty Bud.

"As if a few isotopes would hurt me. I come from solid stock."

"I wonder what your mom would say if she heard that."

Ryker winced. The last time someone implied his mother was less than svelte, they spent a few days healing from the beating she gave them. Mother was a touch sensitive about her weight. "You're getting off topic. I want to know more about this witch."

"Why? You're not planning to see her again, are you? I think she made it pretty clear where you stood."

"Can't say as I blame her. I'm not exactly at my best." Understatement. He currently looked like a homeless slob. The next time he ran into her, and he would, he'd make sure to make a better impression because for the first time since he'd left his parents', he felt like smiling again. And he owed it all to one sassy witch.

Like it or not, we will meet again. And next time, I'll be ready for her.

4

The brisk ride through the late night sky, the stars lighting her way as she flew on her bristle broom, did much to cool her anger. Alone, she couldn't help but replay, with a snicker in her mind, how she'd dumped the cocky shifter on his ass. The look on his face? Priceless.

Men were all the same. Always assuming women were weak creatures who would drop their panties with any crude pickup line. Not her. She preferred a man with manners, grooming, and if he wasn't model good-looking, at least a modicum of sense so they could converse without her wanting to rip out his tongue and shove it where the sun didn't shine. Of course, what she wanted and what she got were two different things. A reputation like hers was a great thing, except when it came to dating. Who wanted to claim a wicked witch as a girlfriend? Who wanted to date someone who could turn them into a roach if they pissed her off? Who wanted to love a woman who could not only take care of herself, but would do so with an evil cackle and true pleasure?

Wicked or not, though, don't I deserve love too?

Weak of her, she knew, yet she couldn't help the stray thought, a thought she'd pondered more and more lately, especially as plans for her sister's wedding snowballed. Seeing her younger sibling so happy—bleh—so in love—gag—roused something in her. She wouldn't exactly call it jealousy, but it was close. She envied what Isobel found. *Will I ever find someone who accepts me for who I am?*

Once upon a time, she'd thought Derek might. Sure, he didn't exactly provide her with intellectual conversation, but he'd at least given her companionship. Usually in her bed or his, away from curious eyes. They didn't really date, or go out for dinner much. They fucked. He went home. It wasn't the most fulfilling of relationships, but at least it was something, and better than being constantly alone.

But I like being alone. Or so she convinced herself. Who wanted to share their space with a man who would demand half of her closet and drawers? Who would leave his socks on the floor and commandeer the remote? Or worse, expect her to cook. Of course, she chose that moment to recall the dinner at her sister's place as Isobel and her fiancé puttered together in the kitchen, chopping and measuring, sharing laughter and conversation as Evangeline rolled her eyes—secretly hating them for their happiness.

Could she find someone like that? Someone who would share a common interest with her and whom she could talk to with ease? *Someone who will embrace my evil side instead of treating it like a flaw?*

The maudlin direction of her thoughts irritated her and as she coasted down from the sky, aiming for her building, she took her annoyance out on the couple strolling along the sidewalk. Her magic made the sidewalk icy despite the warm evening air. Feet went sliding, bodies crashing, and her lips curved in an evil smile when she heard a woman's voice screech, "Get off me, you giant oaf."

Alighting on her balcony, she swiped her finger across the sliding glass door, disarming her alarm before entering. A witch never left her things unguarded.

Evangeline parked her broom in the front hall closet—yes, the whole broom thing was cliché but practical. It didn't take up much space, she could always find parking, and it never ran out of gas. Of course, on the down side, whipping through the air messed up her hair and was only useful on short trips given the low level of comfort that came with a hard wooden handle as a seat. For longer voyages, she tended to use a shag rug.

Away from prying eyes, she snapped her fingers and dropped the glamor she wore whenever she went out. She'd learned years ago if she wanted people—and other supernatural beings—to take her seriously as a force to be reckoned with, she needed to look the part. Unfortunately, her real life shortness and button nose did not make for an imposing witch, not to mention, who ever heard of a sorceress with full pouty lips? Or as one guy put it, *'Perfect for cock sucking.'* She'd made him pay for that comment with an erectile dysfunction spell.

Draining as a magical glamor was to maintain, she used it and adopted a cold, ice queen persona that people noticed. One glacial glare and people knew to get out of her way. She quite enjoyed her alter ego; tall, strict looking with a great set of legs.

Kicking off her pumps, she padded barefoot into her living room, the clear spruce wood floor hidden partially by a thick white shag rug. She loved the open space without knickknacks or clutter, just a pair of matching white leather couches, a large, flat screen television, a slim bookshelf with a handful of magical tomes, and a glass table upon which sat a crystal ball, a ball that currently flashed. Unlike the gypsies and seers, hers didn't act as a portal to view the future; instead, hers acted as a magical version of an answering machine. She only needed to place a hand on it to play back her messages.

"Evangeline, are you there? Hello? Evangeline? Stupid machine. It's your mother, call me."

Beep. Next message.

"Eva! Oh, by Satan's horns, are you never home? You had better be at that dress shop for your fitting on Friday or I am so going to send a demon after you."

Evangeline rolled her eyes at her sister's message. *Not another dress fitting. I'd rather baste for a while over the flames of hell.* Hmm, given who her sister's fiancé was, that could very well happen if she didn't show up. Crap.

Beep.

A high-pitched voice spoke next. *"This message is for Wicked Incorporated. I am in need of the services of a witch of your caliber. If interested in making an obscene amount of money, please meet me at..."*

Evangeline scrambled for a pen and paper to write down the instructions. She recognized both the address and the voice. The speaker wasn't kidding when he said she'd make an obscene amount of money. She'd worked for him before. She wondered what he needed this time. Last time, he'd wanted her to turn a pony into a unicorn for his daughter's birthday, a huge success, even if it resulted in a flood of calls from others asking for more party favors. Of course, most of them had politely hung up when she mentioned her going rate, which didn't bother her, as she had no interest in being some kind of parlor trick for spoiled brats.

As she thought up ways to spend the money she'd soon make, she readied for bed. Alone. *But I could have had some company.* For some reason, the stranger from the bar popped into her head—more specifically the shifter's big, *very* masculine body. What she wouldn't give right now to have that male body with her in bed, naked of course. She'd noticed the bulging muscles that rippled under his clothes. She did so like a big man, problem was they usually preferred someone more delicate than her. Someone like her alter ego. He'd sure seemed interested in getting to know her ice queen persona more intimately. And in retrospect, she couldn't deny she would have enjoyed seeing the behemoth wearing nothing but a smirk.

I wonder if his shaft is as thick as the rest of him. Evangeline very much liked a well-endowed man. Wicked or not, a witch had needs. Carnal needs. Needs sometimes only a man, or at least his cock, could satisfy.

With a squirm of arousal, she slid her hands under the covers and pulled off her damp panties. Masturbation wasn't new for her and would ease the ache in her cleft. Without shame, or a second thought, she slid her fingers through her trimmed curls and found her clit. After wetting her index finger with her own juices, she stroked her sensitive nub and closed her eyes in pleasure. For a naughty visual, she imagined the shifter's heavy frame poised above her, the muscles in his arms tensing as he held himself up, the tip of his cock poised against her sex. He'd dip his head down and suck on her breasts, his unshaved jaw abrading her soft skin.

Evangeline sighed and her finger rubbed more quickly. She slid two fingers from her free hand into her wet pussy, the slickness and heat exciting her. Biting her lip, she imagined the feel of his prick sliding between her thighs straight into her damp sheath, his thickness stretching her and filling her. Her muscles clenched her pumping fingers as her breath hitched. She worked herself faster. Amazing how a fantasy of a complete stranger could excite her. *I bet he's the type of guy who likes to fuck hard, his long shaft driving deep while he sucks on my nipples.*

With a cry of pleasure, Evangeline came, the ripples of her orgasm squeezing her embedded fingers tight. Stunned at her quick bout of self-pleasure, she went to the washroom to wash up, readying herself for a second time for bed. Yet, even after she ran a cool cloth over her heated skin, she still found herself plagued by naughty thoughts of the rugged stranger.

I really need to find a new lover and quick. Look at me, fantasizing about a dirty shifter. I must be desperate. More like horny.

Was it time to lower her standards? At least temporarily? *With my sister's wedding coming up soon, perhaps I shouldn't have dismissed him so hastily.* She did after all know a good pet groomer. Surely they could do something to make him presentable. Shave him. Give him a haircut. Dress him in a suit. Put an electro shock collar around his neck so she could zap him when he got out of line.

And on that thought, and with an evil smile on her lips, she curled up and went to sleep only to have even more erotic dreams about a hulking stranger that had her wet and squirming all night long.

5

"More. Give me more."

Ryker didn't need to be told again. He didn't know how he'd come to find himself between the thighs of the cutie begging him, but he wouldn't deny her what she wanted. In and out he thrust his cock, riding her fast as she panted wantonly, her skin flushed with dew.

He recognized her for who she was. *My mate.* The one meant for him. The one woman who would complete him and accept him for who he was. *My destiny.*

A part of him questioned how he'd gotten her, who she was. Something about the whole thing seemed rather sudden and surreal.

Dreamlike.

A dream.

The illusion shattered and Ryker woke to a raging hard-on, his erotic fantasy dissipating, the details fading, leaving him almost bereft. And still so fucking horny.

Damn it. Couldn't he have woken after he'd at least come?

While his blue balls bothered him, of more intrigue was the lingering certainty he'd seen his mate. Many scoffed at the idea of a predestined lover. He knew he had. Sure, many claimed they'd known from the moment they met their wife or husband that they recognized this would be the person they'd spend their life with. Their soul mate.

Ryker used to call it bullshit. But that was before the dream. Now…now he wasn't so certain. But who was the woman?

Ryker didn't know where he'd seen his dream babe before. Surely, he would have remembered her. Who wouldn't with her brown hair, wild and untamed around her head? Who could forget her button nose sprinkled with a few light freckles and clear greyish-blue eyes? She also had a sweet figure, the kind made to welcome a man's passions. In his dream, he'd fondled full breasts, plentiful enough to spill through his fingers. She'd boasted full, rounded hips, and he dared to hope a smooth, round bottom made for slapping up against. Just thinking about the creamy white thighs from his dream made all the blood in his body converge into one spot—one very hard spot.

Stranger or not, he could so easily picture her when he closed his eyes. She was everything he liked in a woman. Everything he'd ever fantasized.

In his dream, she'd laid on her back with her lush breasts beckoning his hot mouth, inviting and teasing him to taste. Talk about arousing. Ryker's hand closed around his cock and he stroked it, his hand sliding up and down its smooth length. He could almost feel her fingers digging into his scalp as he plucked a tight berry with his lips, sucking it and teasing it with the edge of his teeth. She'd make sweet sounds of pleasure, and she would squirm under him, begging him for more.

He'd oblige. He imagined himself between her creamy thighs, his cock pumping into the wet pussy that welcomed him with tight muscles. His rod thickened even more in his hand as he imagined her legs wrapping around him, locking him tight into her moist sheath. She'd beg him to ride her fast and hard. Clutch him tight to her plentiful tits and rock her hips against him, drawing him deeper, suctioning him with her wet sex...

With a bellow, Ryker shot his load, the force of his orgasm surprising him.

Fuck me. I have to find my dream girl. If this how I come from just imagining her, then I don't even want to think about how it would feel to do it in person. A thought that made his spent cock lift in interest.

Forget the witch he'd met earlier. He needed to find his green-eyed dream babe. His future. His mate.

6

Despite a rather sleepless night—plagued by dreams, nightmares more accurately, centered around a large beast of a man who did unspeakably enjoyable things to her naked body—Evangeline arrived right on time for her appointment. Smoothing down her pristine skirt, she presented an image of poise and professionalism in her black pencil skirt, red silk blouse, and lustrous black pearls. Or at least the glamorized version of herself did. Under the spell, Evangeline wore comfortable black slacks, a snug knitted sweater with a V neckline, and bright red lipstick.

Why the invisible dab of femininity? Surely not because she expected to run into a certain uncouth shifter who, with one skin to skin touch, would see her true self. The chances of her encountering him were practically nonexistent. Since they'd only met for the first time last evening, they obviously did not run in the same social circles. Nor would they again since after the incident of the previous night, she'd already decided to never return to the bar where she'd met him.

Despite her odd attraction to him – and her vastly enjoyable masturbation while picturing him—the reality of his personality—crass—not to mention his caste—disgusting animal—didn't make a relationship, not even a sexual one, a concept worth pursuing. And no, she did not care what her body or subconscious thought. Erotic dreams or not, she refused to abase herself and that was that.

Why was she even wasting time dwelling on it? She had business to attend to and money to make.

Heels clacking on the interlocked paving stones leading up to the grand veranda, she thrust all unnecessary thoughts aside. She'd need her wits about her for her upcoming meeting.

The looming oaken doors of the mansion, eight foot carved monstrosities oiled and stained so that they gleamed, boasted an old fashioned brass knocker in the shape of a gargoyle's head. It opened an eye and glared at her.

"Go away. The master doesn't like door to door salespeople."

"Neither do I."

"He also doesn't entertain light skirts."

Up went a brow. "Do I really look like that type of woman?"

The metallic face sneered. "Nah. You're obviously too uptight."

"I'll show you uptight," she muttered. She pointed a finger at the impertinent creature, and with a zap of magic, sealed its lips shut.

"Mmhphf," it mumbled.

She smirked in reply before grabbing the large ring hanging off the knocker and rapped it sharply off its face. The portal silently swung open and the butler, a rather stately fellow dressed in a suit with the obligatory white, thinning hair and unsmiling countenance, ushered her in.

"Hello, I'm Evangeline Rasputin of Wicked Incorporated. I'm here for my appointment with your master," she stated.

"You are expected. Please follow me."

His back ramrod straight, the servant turned on his heel and led her past vast archways down a marble-floored hall until they arrived at a pair of steel-studded doors. Having been here before, she barely glanced at the magic sigils carved into the metal. Beyond those portals was the owner of the mansion, and a library the likes scholars would kill for.

Not even bothering to knock, the butler let her into the massive home office, currently empty. "The master will be with you shortly." With those words, the servant left, leaving her alone with a priceless collection of books and artifacts. But Evangeline wasn't tempted. She knew better than to peruse, or even touch, without invitation. Evil at heart didn't mean ill mannered. Evangeline respected the privacy of others—unless paid to do otherwise. Besides, curiosity wasn't worth pissing off a client.

While the tomes on display were interesting—*The True Diary of Merlin the Debaucher, One Hundred and Three Undetectable Poisons, How to Satisfy Your Dual-Pronged Demon Lover*—she well knew the really drool worthy items were hidden. A man of prestige and wealth, her client might like to show off, but he also wasn't stupid.

With nothing better to do, Evangeline sat down in one of the leather stitched—by the feel of it, lamia skin—chairs facing the massive desk to wait. The rich and powerful seemed to believe that appointments were something only the lower classes needed to respect. An eccentricity that made her gnash her teeth in exasperation, but which she'd become used to, of a sorts. She passed the time looking around, reacquainting herself with the opulent display of wealth.

Even by her standards, it was obscene from the teak bookshelves—made from only the finest dryad trunks—to the marble desk with its gleaming, polished surface. Her client eschewed modernity, or at least in plain view so there was no computer or laptop marring the slab big enough to use as a sacrificial altar. She should know, she'd attended more than one bloody Sabbath. Her gaze skipped over the familiar array of knick-knacks—all quite rare—that lay scattered around the room. Nothing new popped out. Nothing magical called to her, begging her to take possession, claim its power for her own and go on a maniacal rampage to take over the world.

Oh what a shame. He'd either gotten rid of or locked up the scepter he used to have leaning in the corner. And here she so enjoyed honing her mental skills against the dark, pervasive subliminal message that exuded from its shaft.

Hearing a sound behind her, she quickly stood up and turned to greet her prospective employer, only to exclaim instead, "You!"

Instant irritation suffused her, mixed to her annoyance with a heavy dose of arousal as she regarded the man whose face and body she'd imagined while touching herself the previous eve. Evangeline's lips tightened even as her sex grew damp.

Who the hell let that dirty beast into the house? Mind you, the vagrant had cleaned up since she'd met him. No longer did the beast sport a bristly jaw, wild ruffled hair, and bloodshot eyes. Actually, he was downright gorgeous, something she noticed begrudgingly. *I never noticed last night just how startling blue his eyes were, and thick, ebony hair, made for yanking.*

He looked like a bad boy poster come to life in hip-hugging blue jeans, an open neck black button-down shirt and black boots. In other words, superhot ... except for the sneer on his face. Funny how that expression seemed to follow her wherever she went.

His lip curled back and he drawled, "Well, if it isn't the bitch. Oops, did I slip, I meant to say witch."

Hmm, it seemed his flirtation of the night before no longer applied. Now sober and fully cognizant of the events leading up to his ignoble besting by a mere woman, he didn't seem so attracted. For some reason, this irritated her. "Oh look, a talking animal. Has hell frozen over? I'll have to get my skates sharpened."

"I'd invest instead in a few cases of WD-40 or a blowtorch because you're going to need lots of help prying those thighs apart when you get there, that is if you can find a demon stupid enough to risk your sharp tongue."

Evangeline's nails dug into her palms as she struggled to hold on to her boiling temper. *He might be good-looking, but he's an asshole even sober. If he weren't a shifter, he'd be so dead right now.* She really should start carrying around her ritual dagger for moments like these when only an actual stabbing would do. Then again, she was wearing stilettos…

She took a step toward him, but he backed away with a shake of his head. "Fool me once," he said with a tsking sound and shake of his finger, "shame on me. But it won't happen twice. You might have caught me by surprise last night at the bar, but I'm completely sober now and wise to your tricks. Unless you just can't keep your hands to yourself because we both know I'm irresistible, in which case have at it," he said, spreading his arms wide and inviting her to touch.

A surge of lust almost took her breath away even as her vision turned red. Evangeline rarely lost control of her temper, but something about the shifter drove her absolutely nuts. As if possessed, she found herself stepping forward, her hand swinging to slap the smug grin off his face.

A calloused hand moved lightning quick and caught hers before she made contact, the touch of his bare skin sending an electrical tingle throughout her body. It also made her magical glamor waver as his nullifying effect on magic made its presence known. She saw his face register shock as her actual much shorter form became visible. *Stupid shifter disrupting my spell.*

"You," he whispered disbelievingly.

Evangeline didn't understand the look he gave her, one that registered recognition. No one but close family knew her true face.

"Yes me. Who else would I be?" She tugged at the wrist he held manacled in one big hand, but he refused to release her.

"You wear a disguise?"

"I prefer to think of it as business attire," she replied with a toss of her hair. It probably didn't have the desired effect given it sprang from her head in a wild mane of unruly strands.

"I can see why. This is much too tempting."

Tempting? Not something she heard often once guys actually talked to her and she put them in their place. Had his mother dropped him on his head one too many times as a child?

Her confusion over his reaction made her miss his free hand coming to rest on her waist, but she felt it even through her clothes. Like a molten hot brand, the touch of his hand made her knees go weak, and he pulled her unresistingly up against the hardness of his body. And she meant hard.

Evangeline's eyes widened at the evidence of his arousal pressing against her. *This doesn't make sense. I'm not the type of woman men like to seduce.* As she puzzled over this surprise, he threw her another as he pulled her up to meet his lips and for once, she didn't protest, too caught up in the erotic spell he'd cast over her.

Their lips touched and a disturbing sense of rightness clamored through her, one that screamed, *"Mine!"* A foolish thought that she quickly forgot as she lost herself in the sensation of his lips. They rubbed firmly against hers and stoked the fire that burned between her legs. He drew her closer into him, his strong grasp lifting her so she didn't need to crane to taste the sweetness of his mouth. Her body molded against his, the stiffness of his erection pressed against her, and she mewled, frustrated at the layers that separated their skin.

A high-pitched voice startled her from the embrace.

"Excellent. I see you already know each other," said Mr. Rumpelstiltskin as he entered his office.

Evangeline pushed away from the man who'd bespelled her and rubbed her lips even as her cheeks flushed in embarrassment. What came over her? How could she let him manhandle her like that? *And why did I enjoy it?* Angry at her loss of control, she couldn't stop her hand, which rose lightning quick and cracked across the shifter's face. "Pig!"

The well-placed blow didn't budge his thick head, a testament to his solidity. "Funny, a second ago you weren't complaining about my heritage, and it's feline by the way, not porcine."

"Cat, pig, or dog, you're still an animal."

"An animal you obviously want to fuck. Or are you going to tell me you tongue all the beasts you kiss?"

"I did not slip you the tongue."

"No, I did that, but again, I didn't see you arguing."

"Because you were gagging me."

"That's not gagging. If you were, we'd both be wearing less clothes and you'd be on your knees."

Oh my. She couldn't help flushing red at his innuendo. "You're impossible."

"I prefer the term doable. But then again, you wouldn't recognize that seeing as how you're sexually repressed. Lucky for you I've got the cure for that," he taunted, grabbing his crotch and thrusting his hips.

Crude and disgusting—but unfortunately still hot for some sickening reason. Even as she hated him, she couldn't help desiring him. And by all the fires of hell, it pissed her off.

All control over her temper snapped and her hair rose

in a threatening swirl around her head as her power snapped and crackled, begging for her to use it.

"Ooh, is the itty bitty witch getting angry?" he cooed while egging her with beckoning fingers. "Come and give it to me, baby. We both know you can't hurt me with magic."

Maybe not, but she'd not taken ten years of Brazilian Jiu-Jitsu for nothing. Evangeline might have launched herself at him and pulled a chicken wing on him if Mr. Rumpelstiltskin hadn't laughed and clapped his hands, reminding her they had an audience. "Marvelous as this show is, we do have business to tend to, children. But please feel free to resume this once we're done here. Preferably in front of a security camera so I can replay it at my leisure."

Her patron's humor tempered the simmering rage inside her—or at least allowed her to bottle it for later. Taking a calming breath—like her anger management coach taught her before she turned him into a toad— Evangeline forced her face back into placid lines. Now that the shifter no longer touched her, she put her glamor back in place, using it as a shield to hide her emotions. She had business to attend to. *I'll make him pay later. See if I don't.*

The jerk didn't look in the least bit ruffled, although she thought she detected a hint of amusement glinting in his blue eyes. She almost growled and wondered if some of his beastly nature had rubbed off during their brief embrace. To prevent herself from retorting, she bit her inner cheek. Seating herself once more, she folded her hands primly in her lap. The annoying cat took a position leaning against a bookcase, a smug smirk on his face.

Mr. Rumpelstiltskin seemed disappointed at their cool poses. "Giving up so easily? Pity. I've not been so entertained in ages. Well then, since you've decided to not engage in an all-out brawl, I guess we should get down to business. I've obviously called the pair of you here for a job. It requires both of your skills and will be quite lucrative if you succeed."

Work with the filthy cat? Evangeline's brows drew together and she bit her tongue to stop herself from blurting out the first words that came to mind.

However, he broke the silence first. "I am not working with a witch. I don't work with anyone."

"Probably because you have no friends," she snapped back. "But in this case, I agree. I don't require help, and if I did, it wouldn't be from *you*. And my name is Ms. Rasputin, you filthy feline, owner and sole operator of Wicked Incorporated."

For a moment, his eyes changed color and glinted golden as he let his beast rise for a moment. His whole body took on a hulking, menacing look, one that, instead of inspiring fear as he intended, made her shiver in delight. Oh to have that much muscled power and ferocity between her naked thighs. Why did all her thoughts about him have to end up being about sex?

His lip curled in disdain. "Yes, I heard about your unfortunate relation to that bloody Russian wizard. It isn't something I'd boast about."

That's where he was mistaken. Evangeline lifted her chin up. "My grandfather is one of the greatest wizards alive."

"Funny, last I heard being evil didn't elevate a person

to the rank of great. I hear he kills anyone he thinks is a threat. Even those he was sworn to protect."

"He did not," Evangeline shrieked, losing her temper again. "Those are lies. You are so lucky you are a shifter or I'd turn you into a bug and squish you flat for your insults."

"That's it, use magic because you're too chicken to face people on equal footing."

"Equal footing? That's rich coming from a giant goon like you. Do you enjoy using your size to intimidate people? Well, guess what, you don't scare me."

Somehow, she found herself out of the chair, standing toe-to-toe with him—tiptoe because of his height. He crouched down so they could glare at each other nose to nose. Evangeline couldn't help noticing once again the daunting size of him, a titillating girth that dwarfed her. So much muscle…

"Enough!" With a clap of hands that reverberated like thunder, Mr. Rumpelstiltskin drew their attention. "While I am enjoying this sparring match immensely, now is not the time. I have hired you both to accomplish a task and when I say both, I mean it. I am not chancing anything with the treasure I need you to guard. Do I make myself clear, or do I need to hire somebody more professional?"

The rebuke stung and she drew up all of her five and a half feet—five-foot-eight when under glamor—and replied indignantly. "If you insist, I will work with this creature, but only because of my respect for you. However, the pay better be worth it."

"Yeah, Rumpelstiltskin," the cat said with his rumble of a voice. "If I gotta work with the uptight witch, then I'm going to expect a little something extra."

"Oh you will be amply rewarded, never fear."

"I must also insist on having proof that the animal is up to date on his shots." Evangeline shot him a nasty smile.

"It's not my teeth you should worry about. And the name," he said, turning to her with dangerous eyes, "is Ryker."

It figured he'd have a disgustingly masculine name—one that suited him. She ignored him to face their employer. "What exactly do you need to protect that requires the two of us?"

"I need you to guard my most precious possession," said Rumpelstiltskin.

Evangeline wondered what it could be—gigantic gem, magically imbued talisman, priceless scroll...

"Why not use a safe?" asked Ryker.

"Somehow, I don't think she'd enjoy that. Princess, you can come in now."

Evangeline swiveled to look behind her and saw a slip of a girl entering the office with dainty steps. She moved to stand beside Rumpelstiltskin.

"This is my most precious possession. My first born and only daughter, Princess Tina Rumpelstiltskin."

He wants us to babysit? Evangeline had met Tina before at her birthday party, a shy girl who adored her father.

"I am not cut out to be a nanny," growled Ryker.

"Of course you aren't," said the ugly dwarf. "I need you as bodyguards for an upcoming event. Actually, Evangeline, you're already slated to attend, so this will work out well."

Evangeline frowned as she tried to decipher his words. *What upcoming event? I don't go out. The only thing I'm going to anytime soon is...* "Ah, bloody hell, you can't be serious," she blurted. "My sister's wedding?"

Rumpelstiltskin bobbed his head and beamed. "Yes. Did you know they're already calling it the wedding of the century? Rasputin's granddaughter and the prince of Hell, what a match up."

"Your sister is marrying Lucifer's son?" asked an incredulous Ryker. "Talk about ensuring an evil bloodline."

"Shut up," hissed Evangeline. "He's not that bad. Actually, he's surprisingly decent given his parentage. And besides, it's none of your damn business."

Ryker just smirked at her, then turned to face Rumpelstiltskin again. "Why on earth would your daughter need protection at a wedding?"

"Princess, why don't you run along and see if cook has finished those pastries. Papa will be done shortly." With a kiss on his gnarled cheek and a smile, the girl skipped off. Rumpelstiltskin waited until the door shut before speaking. "My daughter needs protection because my cow of an ex-wife," said the dwarf with narrowed eyes, "is supposed to be attending. She still hasn't forgiven me for getting custody of our daughter in the divorce. Claims I tricked her into giving up her first-born. Bullshit, of course. Heidi only ever married me for my money. Just like she only had Tina for more money. But she pissed through her divorce settlement, so now she's crying foul. I've had a seer looking into the paths of the future, and in one of the possibilities she saw Tina being kidnapped at your sister's wedding and used to blackmail me into giving my ex more money. Unacceptable," said the little man, thumping the marbled surface of his desk hard enough that a crack appeared in its polished surface. Despite his diminutive stature, the little man controlled an impressive amount of power. Her patron had started more than one legend, and her troublemaking side enjoyed seeing he hadn't lost his keen edge or strength.

As to the task, it sounded easy enough except for one thing. "Um, I'd love to help, Rumpelstiltskin, but you do know I'm part of the bridal party? My mother would have a fit if I told her I was backing out now." Money or not, Evangeline knew better than to cross her mother, who was in full wedding fever.

"Already taken care of. You'll only be needed by your sister for the ceremony itself and a few pictures. Since they've asked my darling Tina to sing at the ceremony—she has the voice of an angel, you know—she'll be close by for that span of time."

"So what am I needed for?" Ryker interrupted.

"You'll go as Evangeline's escort, of course. The groom's side had a lack of male relatives with all the killing of those in line for the throne of Hell. Therefore, my old friend Lucifer was more than happy to make you a groomsman. He says to tell you he's been watching you with great interest and looks forward to finally meeting you in person." Rumpelstiltskin grinned mischievously as Ryker shifted his feet, looking distinctly discomfited.

The arrangements seemed too neat, too easy. Evangeline didn't trust it one bit. "Wait a second, what if I said I already have a date?"

Rumpelstiltskin arched a brow at her and Evangeline's cheeks warmed. *How does he know I don't?* Then again, his power came from knowing things that should remain secret.

At the sound of Ryker's snort, without turning her head, she shot her foot out sideways and kicked him in the shin. She didn't even try to hold back a smile at his grunt of pain.

"Now as for your fee..." Rumpelstiltskin named a stupidly obscene amount that had both of them nodding their heads. Hell, for that much money, she'd work with a whole gang of shifters.

But a verbal agreement was only the first part. She and Ryker sat down with Rumpelstiltskin to hammer out the remainder of the details. With the wily gnome, it paid to have all the Is dotted and the Ts crossed. Not to mention, they'd have to work fast.

With the wedding only a week or so away, they'd need to scramble to investigate, find some clues, as well as do some reconnoitering of the event venue. As per custom, the bride's family had made all the wedding arrangements using the limitless funds of her sister's impending father-in-law. Given Evangeline's family's Russian roots—and to please their grandfather—the whole wedding, from binding ceremony to reception, would be held near St. Petersburg in the Catherine Palace. Grandfather had originally wanted Alexander Palace, home of his old friend Tsar Nicholas II, but her mother had argued it lacked the extra size and presence the Catherine Palace would provide. How they managed to secure it for use Evangeline didn't ask. Needless to say, the setting would be beyond lavish with the gilded ballroom and expansive with its dozens of rooms and hundreds of invited guests.

This assignment could end up tricky. What fun! She did so enjoy a challenge—and the possibility of violence.

"I trust the two of you can work out the rest of the

details," said Rumpelstiltskin, standing up to the signal their meeting was ended. "I'll want to speak with you both a day or so before the ceremony itself so you can present your plan of defense. In the meantime, please don't kill each other. It is so much more fun to watch you spar." With a snorting laugh, their employer left them, and suddenly, the cavernous office seemed too small, Ryker's presence crowding her.

Awareness, once again, of his body made her flush. She tried to keep her gaze away from him, but something about him just drew her eyes and she once again noted how his jeans molded his muscled thighs. The thickness of his arms and width of his chest teased her. The memory of his kiss, burning hot and oh so arousing, kindled a fire low in her belly. Damn it all if she didn't wet her panties a little at the thought of his agile tongue visiting a place south of her mouth. Good thing her glamor hid her so he couldn't see her flushed cheeks or poking nipples. But she'd forgotten about his other senses.

He sniffed the air and gave her a slow grin. "I smell something *good*."

Fucking shifter can scent my arousal. Time to get out of here before I do something stupid. Like kiss him again. Or worse.

7

Jeans suddenly too snug, Ryker almost grabbed the witch again so he could see his full lipped dream goddess. He'd nearly expired of shock when he'd discovered the witch from the bar and his fantasy babe were one and the same. It had taken a lot of will power not to take her right then and there. The mating urge rode him hard once he realized who she was. It still did.

He could even picture it, her delicious body denuded and bent over, welcoming his hard thrusts. If they'd not gotten interrupted, he wondered just how far he could have seduced her. He could tell by her scent that she desired him, much as it annoyed her. Actually, his lack of control annoyed him too. The woman truly was a witch. But hornier than he'd ever been, he couldn't seem to help himself. He found himself unwillingly drawn to her like a fly to a Venus fly trap, and when the jaws snapped shut...

Damn, I'll bet the pleasure is worth the pain.

Maybe he should try for another kiss.

As if she'd read his mind, she jumped up from the

chair she'd ensconced herself in and departed with a brisk walk. Ryker followed at her heels, wishing she'd drop the fake image so he could see what her real ass looked like. He bet she possessed a sweet jiggle.

His beast, awake and pacing since he'd walked into new client's office and seen her, kept urging him to pounce on her and bite her neck. Not something his inner kitty had ever wanted to do before, probably because he'd never met the woman meant to be his mate.

But a witch? Really? Perhaps he was mistaken and he just suffered from a case of lust. Or intense blue balls. He'd have to find a way to bang the little witch, get her out of his system, and then see where he and his cat stood. Of course, to do that, he'd have to get her alone. And soon before he died of sexual frustration.

"When do you want to get together and plan our itinerary?"

She whirled without warning and he bumped into her. She stumbled and he shot his hands out to steady her, the skin-to-skin contact breaking her glamor spell again. Cute as a button and lips like juicy berries, she looked up at him in irritation. He could have kissed her, and would have if she didn't look like she'd tear his lips off.

Poking him in the chest, she spoke to him through clenched teeth. "Listen, Rumpelstiltskin might want us to work together for the wedding, but that doesn't mean I have to put up with you beforehand too. I work *alone.* You take care of your end, I'll take care of mine, and we'll meet up at the wedding."

"Listen, witch, I'm not crazy about this either. You're not exactly my ideal partner." Outside the bedroom at any rate. "But I am not going to mess this up because you can't control your hormones around me." He intentionally baited her, not very nice of him probably, but he quite enjoyed seeing the color rushing to her cheeks and her mouth working soundlessly. He had something else he would have preferred to see her mouth working on, but he'd take what he could get for the moment.

"Of all the conceited things! I am not attracted to you." She lied without blinking, and really well too. Unfortunately for her, Ryker could smell the truth, and it was musky, not to mention distracting.

"Okay, let's pretend for a second you're not pining for my body, which we both know is untrue. We still need to work together if this is going to work."

"Get over yourself. I am not pining for your body!"

"Liar. Tell you what, how about I prove you wrong and kiss you right now? Wanna bet I can get you to drop your panties and beg me to take you?"

Damn but she brought out his crude side. Unlike any other woman, though, she didn't run away from his crassness, nor did she burst into tears; instead—and Ryker couldn't believe this—she looked at him with something akin to admiration.

"You wouldn't dare," she snarled.

"Try me."

They stared at each other, the air thick with tension, her scent, a mixture of angry ozone and simmering arousal, swirling around him.

Come on, baby. Dare me. Do something. Make me kiss you. Beg me to fuck you. He almost growled in disappointment when she backed down.

"Fine," she said after a moment of silence. "We'll work

together, but no more kissing. Or touching. Now let me go."

Ryker let her loose, surprised she'd agreed so easily. He'd really hoped he'd get to plunder her luscious mouth again. He watched her step away from him and resume her magical facade.

"Oh, would you drop it already?" he said, following her outside. "I know what you look like, so there's kind of no point."

"I happen to like this look," she said coolly.

"What, presenting yourself as a skinny, uptight bitch? Your real body is much hotter."

Using that as his parting shot, he straddled his sport bike, crushing his aching sac. With a twist of his throttle, he shot off, eager to get home to relieve the pressure in his groin.

A part of him wished things had gone differently because despite his adeptness when it came to masturbating, he feared the only cure for his massive blue balls resided between the creamy thighs of one foul-tempered witch.

8

Long after Ryker had disappeared from sight, Evangeline continued to stare down the long drive, caught in a daydream where he turned around and rode back to her. In her fantasy, he wouldn't say anything, he'd act, dragging her onto his lap, kissing her hard before they rode off together to find a place where they could tear off each other's clothes and screw each other's brains out.

So vivid, so arousing, and yet at the same time, totally impossible. They hated each other. Wanted each other. Were complete opposites. Sexually, though, he was gasoline to her fire. She'd probably end up having to kill him. She just didn't know if she'd sate herself with his body before she ended his miserable existence. A conundrum for sure.

The man is so goddamned annoying, but by the hag's third warty tit, he is also freaking hot.

When he'd issued the ultimatum to work with him or he'd kiss her, she'd almost closed her eyes and pursed her lips. She could lie, more than usual at any rate, if she tried to deny how much she'd enjoyed their interrupted embrace. But getting involved with him? Pure madness.

Mother would have a kitten if she found out I was dating a shifter. Then again, I don't really want to date him, just have wild, raunchy sex with him.

Witches and shifters did not mix. An even better question; why on Earth would she even consider getting involved? So what if the attraction seemed mutual? He had as little respect for her as she did for him. Not to mention his whole dominance problem.

Evangeline enjoyed being in control. Somehow, she didn't see Ryker catering to her. No, he appeared as the kind of who took. Overpowered. Imposed his will—especially in the bedroom. She shivered with arousal.

This wouldn't do at all.

Realizing she stood outside of her employer's house, lusting after her temporary partner, she called for her broom, which she'd stashed behind some bushes. It zipped up and she climbed on board, the wooden handle rubbing against her sensitized bottom. But squirming on her transportation for a cheap thrill while in plain view? Not happening. She'd wait until she got home to take care of *business*.

Casting an invisibility cloak, she flew through the blue sky, blasting the occasional pigeon out of the air—only the stupid or bird-brained dared cross her path. Despite this distraction, her thoughts still strayed toward lusty fantasies involving the oversized shifter.

I need my vibrator—the really big one—right now.

Or she could get to work. With only a few days to plan and investigate, she'd have to pull in a few favors and work overtime if she didn't want to encounter any surprises.

Since greed, usually in the form of money, was the root of most evil, she decided to investigate that aspect first. And she knew just the person to harass for help.

"Hello, little sister."

Isobel screamed before whipping around clutching her chest, immaculate as always in a prim button blouse and pearls with her hair tucked into a casual chignon. Perfect on the outside, yet a Rasputin at heart. "Holy fuck, Eva. Give me a heart attack, why don't you. You are lucky I didn't blast you to bits."

"As if you could. We both know your magic isn't on par with mine." Evangeline flipped her hair and buffed her nails.

"Maybe not usually, however, Chris gave me a present. See this?" Her sister dangled a charm bracelet at her. "Made by Lucifer's sorceress herself. It augments my power."

"Really?" Intrigued, Evangeline leaned forward for a closer peek.

Isobel snatched back her arm. "Get away from it. You are not getting your claws on it, sis."

"I don't need gaudy jewelry to aid me."

"Says the girl who wears a glamor. I swear I could shake you for being so stubborn. You look perfectly fine without it."

"I wouldn't talk, or does the hair on your head suddenly match that of your pubes? On second thought, don't answer that. I do want to know, however, why you're not taking more care with yourself."

"What do you mean?"

"You're the future bride of the antichrist."

"His name is Christopher."

"Whatever. Given who he is, and who you are, no one should be able to sneak up on you. What if I were an assassin? Or a kidnapper looking to take you hostage in an elaborate scheme to blackmail the heir to Hell?"

Arching a blonde brow, her sister smirked. "First off, Lucifer himself has put protective spells around me that will call a horde of demon guards if anyone dares harm me."

"Yet it let me through."

"Because you're not a threat. You're my sister."

"Doesn't mean I don't want to kill you."

"Are you still pissed about my choice of colors for the wedding party?"

Evangeline glared at her younger sister. "You know I hate pink."

An evil grin stretched across her sister's mien as Isobel replied, "You're not the only wicked one in the family."

A chuckle escaped her. "Don't I know it. I think Hell's in for a surprise when you move in."

"Which won't be right away. Christopher and I plan to enjoy a few years topside traveling and causing havoc before retiring to the pit so he can start taking over some of his dad's duties."

"I look forward to reading of your exploits in the papers. But your future isn't why I'm here. I want you to look up something for me. I need the complete financing history for a certain divorcee."

"You want me to divulge confidential information, break some laws, and give you possibly incriminating details?"

"Yes."

"Sounds like fun."

Sweet and innocent appearing on the outside, Isobel was as wicked as they came. And given she was marrying Lucifer's heir, would only get more so. Evangeline almost wiped a tear in pride. All those years of torturing her sibling, playing tricks, and engaging in a competition to prove who could do the wickedest deeds paid off. Isobel caught the eye of the great Lord himself and captured the heart of his son.

And now they planned to marry, not in a traditional ceremony involving church and God-based religions—Grandfather would have gone toe-to-toe with even the Lord of Hell himself if suggested—but in a more appropriate ritual requiring blood, sacrifice, and magic. It also unfortunately involved a puffy pink dress, uncomfortable shoes, and playing nice for a few hours.

Ugh. The things she did for family.

9

After he left Rumpelstiltskin's mansion, Ryker needed distraction else he might have done something stupid such as flipped his bike around and ridden back to abduct a certain curly-haired witch. Sure, he disliked her —she was rude, arrogant, not to mention a witch. But, some of her actions were caused by his behavior. He did kind of do it on purpose to drive her nuts by verbally sparring with her and making outrageous suggestions. What could he say? She was cute when she got riled up. Cute and sexy. A part of him understood it was wrong to want to put her irritation with him to good use and have angry sex with her. And then make up sex. Followed by some sensual sex. And...

Talk about a bad case of lust abetted by his inner feline. Finding himself fighting on several fronts, he did the only thing he could in such a dire situation. He went to Barry's bar.

A beer while on a case? It seemed like a dereliction given the tight timeline on his newest job, however, while the draft ale he ordered in a schooner-sized mug was to help with his witch dilemma, the information he gleaned from Barry would hopefully aid him in his case. Multi-tasking at its best.

"Tell me what you know of Rumpelstiltskin," he asked after chugging half his mug first to take the edge off.

"Can I ask why first?"

"He hired me to do a job. I want to know who I'm dealing with. All I know is he's been around for a while. Has that story about him about spinning straw into gold and trying to bargain for some queen's kid. Oh, and that he's one ugly fucking gnome."

"Gnomes are smaller."

"Then what is he?"

His friend shrugged as he towel dried some glasses. "Fuck if I know. He's one of a kind, that's for sure."

"No kidding. And loaded from what I saw. What can you tell me about him?"

"Keep in mind, most of what I know is rumor."

Rumor with a grain of truth. "That's fine. Spill."

"Well, first off, the dude in the stories, the one who made that bargain? Supposedly, that was his great-great-granddaddy."

"So he's named after him."

"All the males in their line are. Or again, so rumor states. No one has ever actually met any of the boys when young. One day, a younger version just appears and the elder one is gone."

"Patricide?"

"Possibly. Or as soon as the heir is ready, the old guy steps down and retires into obscurity."

"And no one knows what he is? Could he be some ugly fairy?"

"One, there are no ugly fairies. And two, not only does he lack the ears, he doesn't have the wings either. Trust me, people have tried over the years to figure out what group he belongs to, but no one came up with a definitive answer."

"But he's got magic."

"Lots of it. Enough to hide his true self if he wanted."

"So he could be a giant pink demon for all we know."

"In theory."

"I shook his hand."

"I take it he stayed the same."

"Not even a glimmer. If he's wearing a glamor then it's one strong enough to withstand a shifter's touch."

"Interesting."

"Interesting to you, tells me nothing."

Barry shrugged as he put the clean glasses away under the bar. "What do you want from me? I'm not going to make up shit. I told you I didn't know much. The guy keeps to himself."

Not getting anywhere with his current line of questions, Ryker changed tracks. "His daughter seemed human enough."

"Probably because she takes after her mother. I'll admit, I'm surprised you got to meet her. He usually guards her from the outside world."

"She's part of the job I accepted," Ryker admitted.

"Better not fail. Rumpelstiltskin is not one to forgive. And from what I hear, he dotes on his little girl."

"I always deliver. What do you know of the mother?

You said she was human. Is she a witch? Descended from anyone I should know of?"

Barry shook his head. "As normal as they come if longer lived and well preserved. He met her back in the beginning of the nineteenth century. But she looks like she's not older than thirty-five. Gossip in the henhouse claims she used to run in some dark magic circles, add to that the artifacts she no doubt collected during her marriage with Rumpelstiltskin and you've got a woman who might be prepared to do just about anything to stave off age."

"So she might be into magical versions of Botox?"

"I would have called it more along the lines of cell rejuvenation, but yeah."

"Is she hot?" Ryker idly asked.

"If you like the bottle blonde, cougar type."

Not really. He preferred short and feisty with hair that looked like she'd just tumbled out of bed.

His bed.

"Why did she and Rumpelstiltskin divorce?"

Barry shrugged. "The usual according to rumor. She got too demanding. He tried to rein her in. She stepped out of the marriage. Got caught and the husband divorced her. She's lucky. Guys like him don't take kindly to being made a fool, and yet he generously gave her quite the settlement from what I heard. But I also heard she pissed through it and is looking for husband number two."

"What are the chances she'd try and use her daughter as leverage to bargain herself some extra funds?"

"Hard to tell. I've never met the woman myself. From all accounts, she essentially ditched the kid once she and

Rumpelstiltskin split, but I don't know if that was by choice or not. He had some kick ass lawyers on his side."

"Anything else you can tell me?"

"Not really. Like I said, the dude is rich and powerful. He keeps to himself and doesn't like people messing in his business."

Ryker shoved his empty mug in Barry's direction. "Fill me up and tell me what you know about this wedding coming up between Rasputin's granddaughter and Lucifer's son."

"Oh no, do not tell me you're involved in that."

"Involved? I'm an honorary groomsman." Beer overflowed as Barry gaped at him.

"No way."

"Way."

"Unfucking real. You get yourself involved in the most messed up shit. You do know they're already calling it the wedding of the century. A match made in Hell. The biggest event since the birth of the antichrist."

"So it's a big deal?"

"Big deal? Everyone who is someone is going. The guest list alone is the who's who of the evil underground and the neutral. Heck, even the forces of good are planning to attend. No one wants to miss this thing. Except for God, of course. He and Lucifer are still not talking."

The casual way Barry talked about biblical figures that everyone knew existed but no one ever actually met wigged Ryker out somewhat.

"Have you met Lucifer or his kid before?"

"Me? No. He doesn't come topside often and when he does, he tends to drink at his daughter's bar in another state."

"He has a daughter? You know what? I'm getting off track. So this wedding is a big deal. Lots of security then, but at the same time, the potential for catastrophes with so many magical folk in one spot is astronomical."

"I guess. Although, only an idiot with a death wish would do anything to ruin it. Between Lucifer, the mother of the bride, and Rasputin, anyone who fucks it up is sure to suffer an eternity of torment. But why all these questions? Exactly how and why did you get roped into this wedding?"

"I'm supposed to protect Rumpelstiltskin's daughter."

"So you're a bodyguard."

"Of sorts. Me and the witch—"

A frown knitted Barry's brows together. "Which witch?"

"The wickedest one of course. We're going to be working together to figure out who might be targeting my client's daughter and preventing anything from happening."

Barry laughed so hard, he ended up wiping tears.

It was Ryker's turn to frown. "I don't see what's so funny."

"I knew you were depressed, but dude, I never realized you were suicidal."

"One, I am not depressed." Not anymore. "And two, I still don't see what's so fucking funny."

"Nothing. Everything. Here." Barry slid him a shot glass filled with an amber liquid. He topped up a second one and held it in the air. "A toast."

"To?"

"To having known you. I'm going to miss you, old friend, when you're gone."

Ryker made sure to snag the shot glass before socking Barry in the nose and knocking him flat on his ass. As he downed both burning shots, he began to wonder if he should have demanded more money.

Or made sex part of the bargain.

Then again, the idea of courting danger, meeting some legends, and spending time with the witch pushed the last of his moroseness to the side.

It was good to feel alive again. Alive and ready to rock and roar.

10

The following day, around midmorning, as Evangeline chewed on an almost burnt bagel smothered in cream cheese while watching the news—nothing like a series of disasters to start the day—her crystal ball flashed, signaling an incoming call. According to her call display, projected on the wall in dripping red script, the number was unknown. But she didn't have a magical phone for nothing.

Peering into the milky depths of her orb, she gnawed at her lower lip and her body thrummed in excitement, for there in living, scrumptious color was the jerk who wouldn't leave her thoughts—or fantasies. She took a moment to absorb his appearance. Still as rugged as she recalled and just as panty-wetting. It seemed he still possessed an unfortunate effect on her. She licked her lips, thankful that he couldn't see or smell her irritating arousal.

Should she answer? Her body screamed yes, so her mind said no.

She let the call go to voicemail, and barely restrained a shiver at his velvety baritone when he spoke to her magical device.

"Listen, little witch, I know you're home screening your calls. I'm going to be outside of your place in ten minutes. I've got an appointment of sorts to meet with Rumpelstiltskin's ex. I thought you might want to be present for the interrogation. Be downstairs, ready to come with me or I'll assume you want me to come upstairs. And if that happens, I promise I won't leave until you're screaming my name and clawing my back."

Evangeline almost went cross-eyed at his words. *He is the most uncouth, disgustingly hot man I've ever had the misfortune to meet. And damn me if I'm not tempted to have him come up and let him fuck me senseless.* She'd never met a man who made her blood boil and not just with anger. He made her want to do wicked things—with him.

"The clock is ticking," he said before hanging up.

Shit. With little time to spare, Evangeline ran for the bedroom and the vibrating egg she kept in her nightstand. No way was she going anywhere with him without taking care of herself first. She wouldn't allow something as primitive as lust to make her lose control again, at least not around him.

She wiggled her pants down enough to stick her hand with the egg between her thighs. Slick moisture met her, a natural lube for her toy. As she rubbed the vibrating sphere against her clit, she shuddered, recalling his words. *"...until you're screaming my name and clawing my back."* Damn that sounded hot! Evangeline began panting as she stroked herself even more quickly. If only she could let go of her dislike of his kind long enough to screw him, to just feel for once his big, muscled body and taste some of the animalistic passion she sensed in him. Even better, she'd love to have him fuck her, to slam his surely thick cock into her welcoming pussy, thrusting and pumping her to climax. Driving into her. Filling her. Stretching her. Claiming her.

With a cry, her mini orgasm washed over her, leaving her smiling and sexually relieved.

And with five minutes to spare. Quickly, she began righting her clothing. Thoughts of him hummed in her mind as she erased the traces of her mini masturbation session. He thought he was so hot with his big, sexy body. Thought he knew her so well and that she'd just fall at his feet, begging him to take her. Ha. She didn't need him to satisfy her. She could take care of herself.

Wrong. Unable to dispel his image and anxious that she'd soon have to spend time with him, her body tingled. Her pussy quivered. Moisture pooled, creaming her fresh panties.

A scream of annoyance left her. Dammit, her self-pleasuring precaution had only lasted thirty seconds. *Fuck me. I'm getting horny again already.* Maybe he wouldn't notice.

Or maybe he'll take it as an invitation, throw me over his shoulder, cart me upstairs, slam me up against a wall, and screw me senseless.

Where the hell had she put her egg?

11

Ryker straddled his bike outside her building and watched the entrance while mentally counting down. He really hoped she stayed up there because his blue balls were screaming for a cure, a cure that had her name—or even better, her lips—written all over it. His cat, in its prison of flesh—AKA his body—wasn't even bothering with subtlety. It wanted the witch *Now!* Ryker ignored its demands. Despite his niggling suspicion that his feline's actions meant she was his mate, he remained uncertain. She wasn't a shifter. Surely the whole mating thing didn't apply. Maybe he suffered from something else. Maybe he'd caught some kind of sickness. Eaten something along the lines of catnip, which made him lust after the sorceress.

Certain there had to be a reason for his lust, and desperate, he'd done a stupid thing. He'd asked his mother why his inner beast wanted to bite the witch.

Yeah, that had *not* gone well. Ryker hoped she would reassure him that it was some kind of dominance thing, but when his mother went quiet on the phone and said, "Don't you dare under any fucking circumstances bite the witch," he'd quickly grasped the truth, a truth he'd stupidly tried to deny. For some unfathomable reason, his inner beast had settled on the witch for their mate.

And that's just fucking nuts. We don't even like each other, not to mention the whole different species thing. However, even without his beast's urging, he couldn't get Evangeline out of his mind. Each thought of her woke his beast and put it in a frenzy, not only that, but he also ended up with an instant erection. No amount of jerking off helped. He only had to picture her, think of her, and *wham*. Off he went for another cold shower and a five finger session.

Knowing the urge to bite her and make her his would only get stronger and stronger, he tried to stay away. Really, he did. He locked himself in his apartment the night before with a few cases of beer, hoping to drink himself in a stupor. Instead, he ended up outside, wandering the streets, yowling like a randy tomcat. The only reason he'd not ended up outside her window begging entrance was because he didn't know where she lived. A quick call to Rumpelstiltskin's office the following morning solved that dilemma. As soon as he'd written the address down, he'd wanted to tear it up. Fearful he would, his damned cat memorized it.

He threw himself into work, making plans to question people in connection to the case. Got on his bike to go meet them in person. Ended up detouring and giving the witch an ultimatum to join him.

Why? Why did I do that?

Why? Because he just couldn't fucking help himself. He had to see her again. Fighting the urge seemed to make the craving worse. Perhaps if he confronted it, confronted her—by inserting my dick in a hole, any hole—he could get her out of his system so to speak. Or at least relieve the pressure in his balls.

Then bite her, his beast added.

No biting.

He could have sworn his other half laughed. Not reassuring.

When she came down the stairs with less than a minute to spare, he caught himself clenching his teeth. He'd really hoped she'd take him up on his threat and make him come upstairs. He'd even imagined it; his witch bent over, naked, her rounded plump ass up in the air, tempting him as she begged him to fuck her harder. Something he'd gladly do as he cupped her plentiful tits.

Oops. Almost drooled there. He clamped his lips tight.

She'd made her choice clear. Wearing that stupid glamor he hated so much, she emerged to greet him, appearing cool and indifferent. Dammit.

His irritation lasted only until he smelled her. Then he fought his feline for control, and himself because he just wanted to throw her over his shoulder and run back up the stairs with her until he found a bed, or any spot with a touch of privacy. *The little witch pleasured herself before coming down. I don't know if I should be pissed or flattered.* He knew his balls were keenly disappointed, even as his beast purred in satisfaction. *I guess I should be glad to know I have an effect on her.* Because he didn't doubt for a moment she'd masturbated to his image. If she suffered even an ounce of the same attraction then he'd soon have his chance. *If I play my cards right, I'll be plucking—and tasting—her juicy fruit soon, then maybe this stupid obsession will stop.* And if it didn't? At least she'd make his life interesting.

Perusing her through dark-tinted aviator glasses, he smirked. She'd dressed smartly for the occasion in a black pantsuit with heeled boots. She looked every inch the professional. He hoped she'd worn something just as nice under the spell because it wouldn't last much longer.

"You might as well drop the glamor thing now before we run into any humans." Because one touch from him and she'd turn into her true, much more desirable, self.

"I don't want to," she said stubbornly.

"Fine. Have it your way. When you touch me and the real you suddenly appears and freaks the humans out, you can go to the council and explain how your vanity was more important than the rules we all abide by." The council punished severely those who did not follow their number one rule of, "Don't let the humans know."

Scowling, she muttered, "Hate you."

"Ah, you say the sweetest things. Now are you going to change? We need to get going so we're not late."

Looking up and down the deserted sidewalk—not surprising given the yuppies who lived here with day jobs—she let her magical facade disappear and her sexy frowning self came into view. Wearing hip-hugging black slacks, an off the shoulder silky thing that showed off a turquoise tank top underneath, and her hair looking like it got caught in a wind storm, she kicked his horny level up another notch. *Bloody hell, does she have to be so goddamned cute?* Even frowning, she tempted him. Here was to hoping he could handle the upcoming torture of her touching him. Ryker gestured for her to climb on the bike and seat herself behind him.

Eyeing his motorcycle, she shook her head. "I can't get on that."

"Why not?" he asked. "Afraid?"

"No," she retorted. "But I'm not exactly dressed for a motorcycle ride, and I am not wrecking my hair with a helmet."

Wreck her hair? It didn't even look like she'd brushed it. Why did she lie? *Why doesn't she want to get on the bike behind me?* A musky scent wafted, surrounding him. He inhaled deep, savoring it.

Mmmm... *Smells yummy.*

His little witch wanted him. It wasn't her hair or her outfit that kept her from climbing on the back. *She's afraid to touch me.* If it weren't for the worry she'd have an aneurism of rage, he'd have thumped his chest and accused of her of being chicken again. Actually, on second thought, that sounded like fun.

"I know why. You're afraid if you press your body up against mine, you won't be able to control yourself, and you'll maul me. Don't worry. I'm okay with that. Hell, if you want, I'll unbuckle my pants for you now and give you something to hold onto."

He didn't know why he felt the need to render her speechless—or livid beyond belief—but damn, he enjoyed it.

"You are so conceited. I don't know why you persist in thinking you're so irresistible."

"Because I am. Why else would you not want to climb aboard? It's not because you're afraid of speed. You ride a broom. So that means you are scared of getting close to me, proving me right. You want my body."

"Do not. Prepare to be wrong." Glaring at him coldly,

she swung her leg over the seat of the bike and, with no backrest behind her to hold onto, she wrapped her arms around his torso.

Oh hell yeah. Ryker sucked in a breath and almost went cross-eyed with desire. *Mustn't react. Mustn't drag her from the bike and kiss her senseless. Mustn't...*

His beast roared in frustration, which didn't help matters. The sensation of her pressing up against him, her scent of lingering arousal and flowers swirling around him in a heady mix made him wonder if perhaps he'd gone too far. *Fuck her not being to handle it. I don't know how the hell I'm going to navigate when the only thing I want to drive is my cock between her thighs.*

But drive he did, the cool, brisk wind clearing his mind at least. His groin was a whole other problem. Through his side mirrors, he could see her, and what a picture she made with the wind making her cheeks bloom with color. Her sunglasses hid her eyes, but she couldn't hide the way she kept gnawing her lip every time she found herself nuzzling his shoulder.

All too soon, they reached the restaurant. As soon as the bike stopped, his little witch hopped off the bike and in a blink of an eye, managed to look cool and poised, that is if you ignored her wild hair.

Ryker got off the bike more slowly, willing his body to return to a more natural—AKA soft—state. His leather jacket thankfully came down part way and hid the semi-bulge that had taken up permanent residence since he'd begun dreaming of her. No matter how many times he jerked off, as soon as he thought of or saw her, the erection came back.

Raking his fingers through his hair, he gave her a

cocky grin. "Ready, my little *heksen*?" The Danish word for witch came suddenly to his lips as a term of endearment. "Oh and just so you're forewarned, I kind of lied earlier. The ex-Mrs. Rumpelstiltskin isn't exactly expecting us. I thought the element of surprise might work in our favor." He expected her to harangue him over his small fib, but once again, she surprised and delighted him.

"Perfect. Let's go ambush her then." With a smile a shark would have found chilling, Evangeline led the way into the restaurant with the bearing of a duchess. Holding in a chuckle of admiration, Ryker followed, eager to see her in action.

Evangeline unerringly threaded a path through the dining room, brushing off the *maître d'* with a glacial stare that had him backing away with his hands up.

Thumbs looped into his pockets, Ryker followed behind with a feral grin, one which made the patrons in the restaurant give him a wide berth and avoid eye contact. *Why be nice when you can have them fear you? It makes things so much easier in the long run.*

Ryker recognized Rumpelstiltskin's ex from the picture he'd pulled up the previous night when researching her. Blonde and statuesque, she'd modeled for years before marrying Rumpelstiltskin and giving him the one thing he didn't have—a child. Judging by the stones glittering at her lobes, neck, and fingers, it proved a lucrative move. Until she fucked it up.

Without introduction, Evangeline pulled out the seat opposite Heidi, whose ice queen, blonde looks bespoke good old German stock. By all appearances, their employer had stuck to his ancient roots and married from his grandfather's country of birth. Turning a seat backwards, Ryker straddled it, his spot placing him between the two ladies. A great position for him to sit back and watch his witch at work while remaining close enough to intervene in the unlikely case she needed help.

"Excuse me, but that seat is taken."

"Yes, it is. How observant of you."

"I meant that I was holding it for someone else. And that person isn't you."

"How rude. And here we haven't even been properly introduced."

"Who are you?" asked Heidi imperiously.

"I am your worst nightmare if you piss me off," said Evangeline, crossing her legs and flicking at a piece of imaginary lint on her shirt.

"I think you should leave." The blonde raised her hand to signal a waiter.

"I really wouldn't do that if I were you. Answer a few questions, honestly of course, and we'll be gone before you know it."

"And why would I do that?"

"Because you won't like what comes next if you don't."

"You don't frighten me."

A low chuckle left his witch's lips. "I should." Evangeline leaned forward, putting herself in Heidi's space. "But before we get to the reasons why, aren't you curious as to why your ex-husband hired us?"

"You work for Rumpie?" Heidi lowered her hand and narrowed her eyes at them.

"I'm with Wicked Incorporated," said Evangeline, sliding a business card across the table.

Heidi only gave the card a cursory glance. "I have

nothing to say. If Rumpie wants to talk, he knows the number for my lawyer."

"Do you really want to get those barracudas involved? We both know your purse can't handle that kind of expense."

Heidi's lips flattened and her expression turned ugly. "What exactly is it you're after?"

"Rumor is you want your daughter back and are planning to snatch her at a wedding." Evangeline spoke bluntly as she pretended to examine her nails, but Ryker saw through her nonchalant ploy. She'd hoped to catch Heidi off guard. However, he'd wager good money Heidi's surprise was genuine.

"Kidnap that spoiled brat? What the hell would I do that for? He wanted her in the divorce, he got her."

"That's kind of a cold attitude," interjected Ryker. "She is your daughter after all."

Arctic blue eyes turned to look at him, their perusal of his body and the interest that suddenly glinted in them not lost on him, or on his witch, apparently. She stiffened in her seat and her scent suddenly radiated annoyance. Or was the more accurate term jealousy?

"Listen, I might have birthed the girl, but that was the closest we ever were. Rumpie doted on that child from day one and had no use for me after her arrival. His attitude rubbed off on the girl, and she treated me like a piece of furniture—beneath her notice at that. Now let me ask you, why on earth would I want to have her back?"

"More money?" said Evangeline, turning Heidi's attention back to her. "That mansion of yours, as well as your shopping habits, has sucked your divorce settlement just about dry."

"So what? You think I'm going to kidnap my own daughter and hold her ransom?" Heidi's disdain came through clearly. "Please. If I ever touched a hair on that child's head, Rumpie would have me killed, birth mother or not. And as for money, perhaps you should have dug a little deeper. I'm getting married again to a very wealthy man. Something that Rumpie is well aware of. If you're searching for a motive, then you're looking at the wrong person."

Evangeline didn't say anything, but her nails clacking on the table in a rapid staccato belayed her irritation. Rumpelstiltskin had purposely led them in the wrong direction and while Ryker wondered at his motive, Evangeline appeared pissed.

Standing abruptly, his witch made to leave, and Ryker went to follow suit only to halt when the manicured hand of the ex-Mrs. Rumpelstiltskin grasped at his arm and tugged him down.

Giving her a quizzical look, he almost rolled his eyes when Heidi blatantly licked her overly rouged lips and leaned forward, baring her ample cleavage. "Let the witch go and stay with me for lunch. I'm not married yet, and I do so love *giving* and *receiving* dessert."

Ryker didn't have a chance to answer her obvious overture, because his witch, sparks almost literally flying from her green eyes, whirled around. She slammed her hands down on the table in front of the blonde cougar with a resounding smack. Evangeline must have cast some kind of Jedi look-away spell, because despite the loud noise, not to mention the ozone smell rolling off her, she'd not drawn the attention of any of the restaurant's patrons.

"Get your hands off him," hissed his witch.

"Or what?" said Heidi, arching a brow while Ryker struggled to hold back a grin. *Catfight!*

Power sizzled in the air. The static energy made Evangeline's hair ruffle and lift as if moved by an invisible breeze. Her eyes turned almost black as she channeled and held some magic in an obvious power show. "Or I will suck out the youth you've siphoned for years and leave you as desiccated as the mummies in the museum just up the street."

Heidi's eyes widened with fear. "You're a witch."

"The Wickedest Witch, something you'd know if you'd actually *looked* at my business card."

As if Ryker had suddenly developed the plague, Heidi's hand removed itself from his arm and disappeared under the table into her lap. Her face also adopted a more subservient mien. "I'm sorry. I didn't know who you were. I meant no offense."

Ryker wanted to laugh at the way the Heidi bowed before Evangeline's evident power, but he found himself much more intrigued by the jealousy his witch had just displayed.

She might not like me, but she wants me, and I don't get the impression she likes to share. Good. Because he didn't share well either.

12

The smug grin Ryker wore as he trailed Evangeline out of the restaurant had her cheeks burning in unaccustomed embarrassment. She'd made an utter fool of herself. *What the hell possessed me to tell her to keep her hands off? It's not like he's mine.* But while her mind had no problem recognizing that, her body still bristled, a red rage edged in green threatened to rise and she fought the urge to whirl back around and rearrange that uppity bitch's facial features into something Picasso-ish. What a pity magical society rules prohibited petty revenge. Not that she always followed the rules; after all, she'd not gotten the name of wickedest by being a goody-two-shoes white witch.

The biggest problem she foresaw if she did retaliate was the admission that she considered the burly shifter hers. *And I never was good at sharing.*

"Stop grinning," she snapped.

"Who says I am?" he replied smoothly from right behind her.

"I can feel your smugness."

"Can you blame me? You want me."

"Do not."

"Liar."

"Compliments will get you nowhere."

"What will?"

She almost stumbled at his sincere-sounding query. What would it take for her to revert her opinion on him? *Nothing because shifters and witches should mix.* Not even for a few minutes—hours…days…of sex.

Catching sight of his bike outside, Evangeline wanted to groan. *I can't go back on that thing.* She'd barely made it here without latching onto that tempting neck of his and leaving him a permanent hickey. The willpower required to resist on the ride back might be more than she could handle. In an effort to delay, she whipped out her cell phone and dialed Rumpelstiltskin's office.

The line rang a few times and went to voicemail.

"Merrily the feast I'll make, today I brew, tomorrow I bake. The day after that trouble will wake, and all will know whom to blame for Rumpelstiltskin is my name. Leave your message after the tone."

Beep.

"Listen, you little mischief maker, you'd better have a good excuse for why you led us on a merry chase. We know Heidi's not the problem, so either you tell us what's really going on or you can double my rate if I have to go digging for myself." Annoyed, she snapped her phone shut and looked up to see an incredulous Ryker staring at her in shock.

"Did you just give an ultimatum to one of the most

powerful beings in our world?" He sounded almost choked.

Evangeline frowned at him. "He lied. I don't like that. And I meant what I said. If I've got to work harder because he's dicking me around, then he's going to pay for it."

The laughter that came roaring out of him took her by surprise. Most people ran away when she got into one of her black moods. Usually screaming.

"What's so funny?" she asked crossly, not getting his mirth.

He stopped laughing long enough to say, "You have got the balls of a man." Then he roared again.

Compliment or not? Judging by his laughter, probably not. Irritated and aroused at his lack of fear, she wet her lips slowly and sensuously with her tongue. Ryker instantly stopped laughing. His blue eyes glinted with gold as his gaze turned smoldering.

Smiling at him, and pleased at his reaction, she sashayed close enough to put her hands on his chest and tilted her head back to look up at him. As if mesmerized, he simply stared down at her, a move she found unnerving for she could see his beast reflected in his eyes, and it appeared hungry.

"Oh, Ryker," she whispered in a singsong voice, standing on tiptoe.

"Yes," he said, dipping his head down lower.

"I don't like it when people laugh at me." Before he had time to register her warning, she hooked her foot around his ankle and pushed on his chest, toppling him.

Damn his feline reflexes. While taken by surprise, he

didn't hit the pavement as hoped. He recovered with only a slight wobble and Evangeline took a step back because the gleam in his eyes and the tilt of his lips promised retribution.

Uh-oh. She couldn't help but shiver.

He wagged a finger at her. "Naughty little witch. For that, you owe me a kiss."

"You wish."

"Not for long."

"Are we going to do this the easy way or hard way?"

"What's the difference?" Oh how devilish he seemed with the naughty grin that stretched his lips. Evangeline swallowed hard and warm liquid soaked her panties.

"The easy way, you just get your ass here and pucker up. I kiss you. We're done."

"And the hard way?"

"You make me chase you. I get really hot and bothered. I drag you into the nearest alley and show you why you shouldn't taunt men bigger and stronger than you."

"You wouldn't dare."

"Then you obviously haven't done your research. I'm not a tame little boy. Nor do I like to follow the rules. I want a kiss and I will have one. The only choice you have is the how. Make your choice, witch, or I will make it for you."

The usual methods she employed involving magic wouldn't work on him. Damn his shifter genes. And he was right. His size did give him an advantage. She'd really need to look into carrying around a silver dagger to avoid situations such as these. In the meantime, though, she had a choice to make.

Taking his kiss like a woman—and enjoying it—or running and getting even more than a simple embrace.

It seemed she was more cowardly than she knew. She chose to give in to the simple kiss. Only there wasn't anything simple about it. One touch and she wished she'd taken option number two.

13

SHE GAVE IN WITHOUT A FIGHT.

Ryker couldn't believe it when her face softened and her lips parted. An invitation if he ever saw one. Not one to waste an opportunity, especially when he'd expected her to run, he quickly folded her into his arms, her plush frame a perfect fit against him. He restrained himself from crushing her velvety lips, instead tasting them gently, her arousal rising in a musky cloud around them and making his primal instincts come forth.

Inside his mind, his beast paced restlessly, the urge to mate—to *claim*—the woman in his arms almost overwhelming. He molded her body against his, his firm erection pressing insistently against her stomach, but instead of shying from his evident excitement, she dug her nails into his back and squeezed herself closer. He cupped her perfectly rounded ass with his hands as she opened her mouth, her sinuous tongue venturing forth to duel with his.

Had sanity not suddenly prevailed in the form of a

catcall—"Get a room!"—and reminded him they still stood—barely—on a city sidewalk, he would have taken her right there and then. He could even picture it. She'd have her pants around her ankles with her rounded tush bent and presented to him. Or, even hotter, he'd sit sideways on his bike, she'd straddle him and ride him, her sweet bottom bouncing up and down on his lap. He'd cup those cheeks, impaling her, while kissing her neck, preparing her for his mark.

Oh fuck!

With a curse, he broke off the kiss and moved back in an attempt to regain control of his hormones. A move his beast disliked judging by its snarl of frustration.

The man wanted to snarl, too, as he saw her eyes heavy-lidded with desire and her lips swollen and inviting. However, she deserved better than a public rutting—well, at least not for their first time. *So, what the hell am I waiting for? Let's get her back to my place. She is ripe for the plucking.*

Straddling his bike, Ryker held his hand out to her. Asked her without words to come and finish what they started.

She swayed where she stood, her eyes blurred with passion, her lips red and full from the kiss, her nipples hard points through her thin shirt. Indecision warred on her expressive face. He gestured for her to join him on the back of the bike and in return, his bed, but she shied back on unsteady feet.

Her forehead creasing, he saw the passion in her eyes fade, replaced with reality. That never boded well.

"Come with me, Evangeline," he said, still hoping she'd let her hormones do the talking. Fat chance.

Adopting a smooth, expressionless mask, she hid the remaining signs of her capitulation to him. "And just where do you want to take me?" She couldn't hide the breathiness in her voice and Ryker inwardly smiled. She could pretend all she wanted. He could still smell her arousal.

"I don't suppose you'd like to see the ceiling in my bedroom?"

Expecting the slap that came flying his way, he caught her hand and used it to jerk her close. Again, unlike any other woman who would have been frightened by such rough treatment, her eyes smoldered with restrained passion. "Pig. Just because I enjoyed the kiss doesn't mean I am going to screw you."

"I don't know why you keep stubbornly denying the chemistry between us."

"Because you're an animal."

"I am. In and out of bed. And if you ask me, I think that turns you on."

"Arousal or not, I won't be looking to you for the solution. There are other men out there suitable for the task."

Did she just threaten to fuck another guy? Oh hell no. He couldn't help the menacing growl. "Don't you dare."

"Or what?"

"Or you'll see what happens when you piss a large cat off."

"What I do in my spare time and with who is none of your affair."

"That's what you think." Before he did something stupid, in plain sight of curious humans who watched their altercation, he kicked the parking stand off his bike and turned the key in the ignition. "This isn't over, witch. I'll be seeing you—*all of you*—soon."

He gunned the bike before peeling away from the curb, a jealous rage simmering along with ball-aching arousal.

Cold shower and five-fingered shag, here I come.

14

Late again. It seemed she'd spent the last few days arriving everywhere late. Getting started on her day late. Going to bed late. She who hated tardiness, now the queen supreme of it.

This is all his fault. Him and that damned kiss.

The hottest, panty-wetting kiss and the fact he kept calling and calling. Cajoling her to meet him. Threatening to come see her. Sensually asking her to let him in. Demanding she answer.

Idiot that she was, she kept replaying his messages over and over. Sometimes masturbating to the sound of his voice. Other times standing with chattering teeth under a cold shower spray. Nothing she did could stop the temptation he posed. The arousal he evoked. The longing she couldn't stem.

This turmoil and the solutions she kept attempting screwed with her time management. Case in point—he'd just called, again, describing in vivid detail what he'd enjoy doing to her body.

Forget the fact she was expected for a dress fitting, her body required attention. Not that it helped the underlying problem.

I want him.

And she didn't think she had the willpower to fight it any longer.

Walking into the bridal shop, she wondered for the umpteenth time why he hadn't come knocking on her door—or kicking it down—as her body had avidly hoped he would do. Did he have some kind of shifter code that wouldn't allow him to force entry? Did his pride demand she capitulate? A better question was, *what would I have done if he had shown up in all his masculine glory?*

Too easily, a vision came to her of licking her way down his chest, following a triangle of hair that led to...

Damn, another pair of fucking panties to wash. Stupid, oversized... She didn't even realize she grumbled aloud until her sister Isobel said, "Who's too hot for his own good?"

Blushing, a much too common occurrence nowadays, Evangeline glared at her sister, whom she'd not even noticed, too caught up in her own internal ranting. "No one."

"So Mr. No-one has you threatening to drop his hot ass in a South Antarctic crevice?"

Unfortunately, her mother and sister had both insisted she go au naturel to the wedding, which meant she couldn't hide behind her usual mask. "It's nothing."

"Doesn't sound like nothing."

"Just some annoying stalker guy who won't go away. Don't worry about it." Figured her sister would note her heightened color as she tried to avoid replying.

"Ooh, have you been hiding things from me, Eva?"

Evangeline scowled, which only deepened Isobel's grin. "Can we just get this over with? I have a job I need to do some research on."

"Wow, whoever he is, he's really got your panties in a twist," said her shockingly beautiful—*and skinny, the bitch*—sister. "Anybody I know?"

"No." A statement she had to revise given her upcoming job. "Kind of. He's a groomsman and he's going to be my partner for the wedding."

"Oh, the man Rumpelstiltskin wanted you to have to help you guard his little girl."

"You know about the job?" said Evangeline, surprised. She'd assumed her mother would keep it a secret so as to not stress Isobel before the wedding from Hell.

"Of course I do. Christopher and I don't keep secrets from each other," said Isobel smugly.

So it wasn't Mother who tattled. Of even more surprise was Isobel's belief that Christopher didn't belong in the same category as every other lying, scum-sucking male on the planet. *I mean, come on, my sister's fiancé is the heir to Hell.* But hey, if it made her happy to believe he told her everything, Evangeline wouldn't ruin it. She might act abrasive with her sister, but the truth she'd deny if anyone asked? She loved her sibling deeply. Although she'd kill anyone who suggested it. She did have a reputation to maintain.

"So is he hot?" asked Isobel, twirling in front of a mirror and admiring the flowing line of her cream-colored wedding gown. At least she'd not gone with a classic white. One thing her sister certainly wasn't, since meeting the prince of Hell, was a virgin.

"Who is hot?" asked her mother coming from the back.

"No one," mumbled Evangeline, wishing her sister would take the hint and STFU—shut the fuck up. Not likely.

"Eva's got the hots for some guy, and he's coming to the wedding," tattled Isobel, who stuck out her tongue when Evangeline flashed her the middle finger.

Her mother's eyes widened. "A man. Evangeline, are you keeping secrets? Who is he? What class of magic does he dabble in?"

"He's a pain in my ass and he's not a wizard or sorcerer, so you can get that matchmaking gleam out of your eye, Mother. We're doing a job together, and once it's done, he is out of my life."

"But if you like him—"

"I do not like him," yelled Evangeline.

"Then why were you blushing?" taunted her sister.

"I don't want to talk about it." Evangeline grumbled under her breath about nosy sisters and interfering mothers as she grabbed the hanger with the pink monstrosity they expected her to wear and headed for the changing rooms.

She stripped out of her clothes and stood in her bra and panties, scowling at the frilly bridesmaid gown. Knowing she only delayed the inevitable, she struggled to get into the dress, the filmy layers battling her at every chance.

"Stupid, frilly, ugly, pink." On and on she cursed the bloody gown. When she finally wedged it on, she reached and strained, but to no avail. She couldn't do up the zipper at her back

"Evangeline," called her mother. "What is taking you so long?"

"I can't do up the stupid zipper," she shouted back.

She heard the curtain behind her rustle as someone stepped in, but the electric shock that ran through her at the touch of the calloused fingers at her back let her know it wasn't her mother or sister in there with her.

Whirling, she gaped at Ryker, not really surprised to see him. Her body had instantly known, and honestly, she'd expected to run into him before this.

"What are you doing here?" she hissed even as a tingling awareness ran through her body.

"Well, you avoided all my calls, so I contacted your mother, who was most helpful in letting me know where you'd be today."

Her mother who'd just a moment ago acted as if she knew nothing about Ryker. Devious old sorceress!

"You need to leave now." Evangeline felt her heart rate speeding up. It had been two days since their last encounter and apparently, absence made the body hornier. Her knees grew weak and heat suffused her body, especially in the damp spot between her legs.

"I am not going anywhere. As soon as this dress fitting is done, you and I are sitting down and hashing out our plan. Actually, first, I am going to fuck you until you scream my name. Then I am going to fuck you until you claw my back. Then, over some take out, we'll hash out our plan."

Oh, dark lord, did he have to say it in such a demanding way? "And if I say no?" Evangeline didn't have it in her to cave so easily.

"You won't." Before she could move, his hands were on

her waist and lifting her up. She should have protested, kicked him in the jewels, done something, but all she could do—and really wanted—was to close her eyes and tilt her head up toward his.

The hard lips crushing hers did not disappoint. Ryker kissed her with an urgency and passion that matched her own sexual frustration. Under his questing tongue, she parted her lips, eagerly meeting his sensuous thrusts with slippery stabs of her own. He tasted just as wild as she recalled. And oh how he fueled her burning desire.

The strength he displayed as his hands held her tightly and effortlessly off the floor made her melt and also made her mouth all too easy to plunder. She clutched at his muscled shoulders, wanting to tear the fabric that stood between her and the hot flesh hidden beneath.

"Evangeline, hasn't your man helped you zip up yet? You've been in there a long time. What are you two doing?"

"What do you think they're doing, Mother?" Isobel said, laughter in her voice.

"What do you mean? Oh. *Oh!*" Her mother's shrill voice acted like a cold bucket of water. Evangeline froze in Ryker's embrace. With a sigh, he set her down.

"I've really got to pick better spots to kiss you," he said in a mournful tone she totally understood.

Evangeline stepped back, trying to regain some semblance of equilibrium, a difficult task with his body temptingly close. The small cubicle had nowhere to run, though. The bench behind her made her stumble, and she sat down hard on its surface.

Befuddled and aroused, she looked up at his enigmatic face with his hooded eyes, the gold in them glinting, showing the passion that still simmered just beneath the surface. Down dropped her gaze to his mouth. His wickedly pleasurable mouth, which, only moments ago, possessed hers. She licked her lips. With a soft curse, he dropped to his knees in front of her.

"Stop staring at me like that."

"Like how?"

"Like you want me to finish what we started. I can only take so much."

"Then maybe you shouldn't have come."

"I tried. But dammit, I couldn't stay away."

He couldn't? For some reason, his angry admission created a warm spot inside.

"What do you want from me?" she asked.

"You."

Such a simple admission. And probably the sexiest confession she'd ever heard.

"We shouldn't."

"I don't care."

"Eva, I am still waiting. Are you coming out?"

"I think a better question, Mother, is are you decent?"

"Isobel!"

"What? Did you see the hunk that went in after her?"

"You shouldn't notice such things. You are getting married."

"I'm getting married, not going blind."

Evangeline sighed as her family continued to banter. A wry grin tilted Ryker's lips. "I guess I should have chosen a better spot to ambush you. Finish your dress fitting and meet me outside. We'll go somewhere and *talk*. Okay?"

She doubted they'd get much talking done, unless you counted his dick saying hello to her pussy, which at this point was the only conversation she wanted to have. She nodded in silent assent and watched, as with one last cocky smile, he left through the curtain.

What am I going to do about him? I've never wanted a man like this. I turn positively stupid when he's around. Figures the one man who makes me lose my wits is an obnoxious shifter. A passionate animal who could handle her dark side.

When Evangeline knew she could stand without collapsing in a puddle on the floor—that man packed a whopper of a kiss—she exited the change room and immediately faced her smirking sister.

"You're right," Isobel said. "He is too hot for his own good."

Yes, he is, and I want to burn up in his embrace.

15

Ryker sat in the coffee shop across the street from the bridal store, and watched the door, still aroused, definitely befuddled, and impatient as hell.

What the hell just happened? Other than the most passionate embrace of his life. He'd simply intended to track her down, since she wouldn't take his calls, and hash out their next plan of action. Instead, at the sight of her looking like a delectable bonbon, he'd kissed her, something both the man and beast had greatly enjoyed. Something she enjoyed. A kiss he intended to finish once she met up with him and he'd gotten her somewhere private. No more interruptions.

It had taken great will power to walk away; something his beast still hadn't calmed down about. The big feline paced the edges of his mind, agitated and growling.

At this point, Ryker didn't know what to do or think. Fighting his attraction to the witch seemed a lost cause. And honestly, the moments of bliss he'd experienced so far with her made him wonder why he even bothered trying. Heck, he'd technically stalked her by phone for the past few days, leaving message after message, trying to demand, entice, beg for a response. She'd not answered. He'd taken to lurking outside her place, but she avoided capture, taking to the air on her damnable broom. In the end, he'd swallowed his pride and cheated by calling her family. Yes, he'd ambushed her. He had to. He could no longer fight his attraction.

He'd gone through the reasons to stay away countless times.

She's not a shifter. Mother will never approve. But then again, he'd tried doing it his mother's way before and look how that turned out. His brothers had done their duty to the clan; they didn't need Ryker to carry on the bloodline. So why couldn't he do what his beast—and the man—wanted?

Was falling for a witch really that bad? He'd always been different from his brothers—bigger, more aggressive, and a hell of a lot more sarcastic. So why shouldn't he be different in his choice of a bedmate too? Sating his desires on her luscious body might put his pacing kitty to rest, not to mention relieve the aching tension in his blue balls. He didn't need to make her his mate. He'd keep it to sex only.

If she didn't change her mind. Oh fuck. He hoped she didn't. He didn't think he could last another day without sinking into her sinfully sexy body.

Ryker must have made a noise or winced because the voice of Evangeline's mother came from in front of him asking, "Is something wrong, dear? You look like you swallowed something sour."

Ryker glanced up with assessing eyes as the woman

who looked like Evangeline's older sister sat down. *It seems witches age just as well as shifters do.*

"You're Evangeline's mother, aren't you? The one I spoke to on the phone."

"Yes, my name is Marya Rasputin, but you may call me Mary. So you are the hot man who has my daughter throwing a tantrum?"

Straight and to the point, just like her daughter. Ryker didn't even try to withhold his grin of masculine pleasure at knowing he had Evangeline in a frenzy. "Funny, I wouldn't have thought tantrums unusual given what I've seen of her."

Mary laughed. "Yes, my Eva can be somewhat controlling and temperamental. She needs a strong man to rein her in. Someone who will not fear her little mood swings."

"Fear her?" It was Ryker's turn to laugh. "She's too cute to be scary."

His words rendered Mary speechless for a moment, and Ryker had to wonder what idiots his witch had dated in the past. He really needed to kill them for touching her.

"I'm Ryker Pantero, by the way. A shifter, in case you didn't already know."

A dark brow arched and she smiled. "A *Pantero*, and I'll bet you're an alpha too. Interesting. No wonder Eva won't talk about you. She has this misguided notion about species not mixing."

"Funny, I was going to say my clan has that same notion."

Mary stared at him intently. "And will that stop you from pursuing what your beast wants?"

Her words startled him. "How do you know about what my beast wants?"

"I am Rasputin's daughter, I know many things. But you did not answer my question. Will you claim my daughter?"

His beast stirred and snarled a reply, a reply he echoed. "Yes." Funny, he hadn't even known his answer until he spoke it aloud.

"And if she says no?"

Ryker turned from the window, the one he kept peering through so he'd catch his witch when she emerged from the salon. He regarded the woman with the odd questions. "Then I will *convince* her." Even if he had to tie her down and tongue her until she screamed *"Yes!"*

Satisfied apparently with his answer, Mary nodded her head and smiled. "So be it. Now you'd better hurry before she runs off on you again."

A quick look out the window showed his witch looking up and down the street, her lower lip clamped between her pearly teeth. *Oh no you don't.*

With a quick "Bye," Ryker dashed outside and hailed Evangeline. She stared at him, her eyes full of such erotic longing that he, the graceful one in the clan, stumbled.

His beast just chuffed—*Mine.* Ryker didn't disagree. *Yes, ours. Ours at last.*

16

"Where do you want to go so we can *talk*?"

She understood what he meant, and lucky him, she'd come to a decision inside the dress shop, one that would see them naked and doing the horizontal tango in less than ten minutes—if he made all the lights between here and her place. *Why fight what my body wants? It's not as if I love him or something. It's just sex.*

"Let's go to my apartment."

The words no sooner left her mouth than they were flying through the streets, his bike weaving among the cars in a dangerous dance that exhilarated her.

She sat behind him with her arms wrapped tight around his torso, her lips brushing his nape, nibbling and kissing until he growled. "You'll get us both killed." With that kind of warning, she latched onto his skin, sucking him as he cranked up the speed in a deadly race to get them to her place.

Once there, she led the way up the stairs to her third floor apartment, his electric presence behind her enough to make her legs weak and wet her already drenched panties.

"Dammit, witch, move faster, or I'm going to take you on these damn stairs."

Startled at his confession, she whirled to face him. Did she really tempt him that much? The idea both excited and confused her. Men did not find her irresistible. They did not act like savage beasts with no control. Until Ryker.

Blazing eyes of gold, passion having swept away almost all signs of the less than civilized man, she found herself swept up in a brawny pair of arms. He then proceeded to jog up the rest of the stairs. His macho man act enabled her to resume nibbling the skin along the side of his neck and jaw. She quite enjoyed the little growls he emitted at each nip of her teeth.

"Keys?" he said, sounding pained in front of her door. Evangeline waved her hand at the portal, which with a few clicks, swung open.

"Nice trick," he said, striding in. She used her magic to push the door closed, and just in time, too, because she lost all reason when his lips came down hard over hers, the force and passion behind his embrace overwhelming in its intensity. It was also highly pleasurable.

He unhooked his arm from under her knees and let her legs down, not that they wanted to hold her weight. Knees weak, Evangeline pressed herself up against his hard length, twining her arms around neck as his wrapped around her, hugging her tight. She moaned into his mouth at the electric feel. Shivered at the bulge pressed against her lower belly.

Pushing her up against the wall to brace her, Ryker's hands tugged at her clothes, which took too long to come undone in Evangeline's impatient mind. With a whisper of magic, she pulled all the stitches out of their garments and the loose fabric dropped to the floor.

"Neat trick," he chuckled. He wasted no time in enjoying their naked status, plastering himself to her, skin to skin. Thank the dark lord, he pinned her to the plaster, holding her up because the friction of his body against hers made her tremble. A boneless mass of sensation, she would have probably slid to the floor. The rough edge of his unshaven jaw scraped across her tender skin as he kissed and licked his way down the middle of her chest. Rough hands cupped her plentiful breasts, his thumbs rubbing against her protruding tips. When he finally sucked a peak in to his mouth? She squealed and clutched at his hair, urging him on, grinding his face against her. He took his time torturing her nipples. Pulling the nubs with his lips. Pinching them with his teeth. Running his tongue over and around them while pressing a muscled thigh between her legs, rubbing it against her core until she writhed.

"Stop teasing me," she gasped. "And fuck me already."

"Are you sure? I could do this all day," he taunted, his warm breath fluttering against her damp nipple.

"I want to come on your cock."

Magic words it seemed. Instantly, he stopped his foreplay and pressed himself to her, his lips scorching hers in a passionate kiss that stole her breath. She could feel his shaft, a hot, living beast, throbbing against her belly.

"Do you have a condom?" she panted, frantic with need, but not so far gone as to forget protection.

"Shifters can't get diseases," was his reply.

Evangeline almost swooned with delight, because she

already knew their different castes precluded pregnancy. And oh how she looked forward to the sinful pleasure of having a man inside her without a latex barrier.

Their lips locked in a kiss that made her blood run molten through her veins. She wanted him desperately. As if sensing her need, his hands cupped her ass cheeks and squeezed before he lifted her off the floor, pressing her back against the wall. Oh darkness, how she enjoyed his effortless strength. Used to coupling in the standard positions, she found the concept of doing it standing up rather titillating. Not that she needed any more stimulation.

Aloft, with her legs straddling his waist, she could easily feel his thick head pulsing at the entrance to her sex. She angled her hips with an impatient mewling sound, tired of waiting. When he probed her with the tip, she exhaled a happy sigh.

Slowly, too slowly for her liking, he slid his hard length into her, and Evangeline dug her fingers into the muscles of his shoulder, awash in sensation.

"Wrap your legs around me," he whispered in her ear. He didn't have to tell her twice. She immediately latched her limbs around him tight, which in turn drove him even more deeply into her. She moaned and tensed, her whole body trembling and on the brink.

Thick, rigid, and long, just like the rest of him, he stretched her deliciously. Filled her up. Filled her up and left her craving more. She could sense he held back.

"Bed?" he asked in a pained voice.

"Too far," she gasped.

He hissed and threw his head back. "I'll make up for this later, I promise." With his fingers gripping her ass cheeks, spreading them, he pumped her tight sheath, long strokes that had her keening and panting. She tried to hold on, to prolong the ecstasy that coursed through her body, but when the tip of his cock found her sweet spot over and over, hitting it, making her shudder, she lost it.

Screaming loudly, she spasmed around his hard length. Her climax rippled and clung to his driving cock and it wasn't long before he yelled and shot fiery liquid inside of her.

Oh dark lord, that was good. More than good. Amazing. Fucking awesome.

Evangeline shuddered, the pleasure in her refusing to abate. Demanding more. *I wonder how long it takes a shifter to recuperate?* Because she was ready for round two.

17

Ryker tightened his hold on his little witch when she shuddered, sending a jolt of pure desire right through him. Unbelievably, he could feel himself growing hard again. As if once with her would be enough. He wanted her again, but this time, he would take his time exploring her instead of ravishing her like a savage beast. And for that, he wanted a bed.

Her soft ass cheeks fit perfectly in his hands, and he squeezed them as he carried her away from the wall where he'd just taken her, no better than a rutting animal in heat. Of course, he hadn't heard her complaining. On the contrary, she'd reacted to his passion with even more fervor than he'd ever imagined from a woman.

Fuck, is she hot. And perfect. And sexy. *And mine.*

"Where's your bed?" He followed the wave of her hand into a room that he didn't even bother to look at. Who cared about the décor when all he wanted was the big bed in the middle of it?

Not letting their bodies separate, he placed her on the

bed, his ever-hardening cock still nestled inside her moistness.

She looked up at him inquisitively, and with a cat's smile, licked her lips.

"Witch, you are some kind of naughty."

"And the problem is?" she asked coyly, lifting her arms above her head, drawing attention to her bountiful tits.

"Have I mentioned I love naughty?" he said before dipping his head to take one of her tempting pink nipples into his mouth.

Her fingers immediately twined in his hair, yanking roughly at his strands. He growled his appreciation around his mouthful and dammit it she didn't arch her back, offering her breast up to his mouth. Practically begging him to do more.

Ring! Ring! Ring!

He could tell she wanted to ignore it. She had her eyes clamped tight.

Ring! Ring! Ring!

Distracted, he pulled his mouth away from her nub and said, "Don't you have voicemail?"

"Yes," she replied through gritted teeth. "But the fact it's not picking up means someone with magical means is doing on purpose to get my attention."

Ryker sighed and rolled off the bed, the sight of her naked splendor enough to make him want to throttle the caller.

Of course, the ringing phone did give him a great view of his shapely witch as she came up off the bed, her creamy flesh inviting as she stalked out to her living room. He swallowed hard as he finally got a good glimpse of her rounded ass.

Now there's an ass I can't wait to slap my body up against. With an erection he could have hung a flag on, he followed her out to her living room area and suppressed a grin when she touched a glowing orb and snapped, "This better be good."

"My dear Miss Rasputin, so nice to hear your dulcet tones. I was returning your call as requested. Is this a bad time?"

Ryker could hear the suppressed mirth in Rumpelstiltskin's voice as he baited Evangeline. Judging by the static lifting her hair, she could hear it as well, and her tone when she replied would have frozen even the hardiest of arctic creatures.

"You lied to me about your ex-wife, Rumpel," she said, not even deigning to use his full name, annoyed with their employer and unafraid to show it. "Now, you do realize this will mean an increase in my fee?"

"Now, Evangeline, it was an honest mistake. The threat I received was vague and I naturally assumed it had to be Heidi. I realize now the error of that assumption. I will of course increase your fee, especially in light of the new information I've received."

"What new info is that?" asked Ryker, speaking up.

"Oh, I see your partner in this task is there as well. How *delightful*."

"Get to the point, would you?" snarled Evangeline. "The wedding is in a few days, in case you hadn't noticed. I don't have time to play your stupid games."

"You really know how to suck all the fun out of things," said Rumpelstiltskin, sounding disgruntled. "Fine. You need to speak to the vampires. I assume you know where their coven is hidden?"

Who didn't? For a race that purported it wanted to be left alone, very few people were ignorant of their lair. But then again, why leave home for take-out when they could get delivery?

"You'd better not be fucking with us again, Rumpel."

"Would I do that?" asked the ugly man in a tone meant to sound hurt. "Try not to let them suck the life out of you." With a cackle at his own jest, Rumpelstiltskin hung up.

Ryker paced her living room, mentally planning their next move. One did not go into a vamp lair without preparation.

"If we're going to visit with vamps, I need to hit my place."

"What for?" she asked, still frowning at her orb.

"If we're gonna make nice with blood suckers then we need to impress them. I have an idea. You coming?" he asked.

"I wish," she said, her voice low and forlorn. Ryker caught her sexual innuendo and for a moment debated saying "Fuck Rumpel" so he could fuck his witch, but then common sense—and an image of all the zeros—brought him back to his senses.

Then again...they didn't need to leave right this second. Night fall was still a few hours away.

"We have a bit of time," he said with a wicked smile.

"We really should be prepping for the vamps."

"Don't worry. We'll be ready by dusk."

Instead of telling her what he planned, he just picked her up fireman style—nearly went crossed-eyed at having her delectable bottom so close to his mouth—and went off to find her bathroom. Turning on the taps, he stepped back to wait while the water warmed and gave in to temptation and nuzzled her cheeks.

"What are you doing?"

"Enjoying the view."

"Liar."

"What's that supposed to mean?"

"I'm well aware I have a fat ass."

"I happen to think your ass is perfect."

"It's too big."

"Just right." He rubbed his cheek against it again. "Witch, if you only knew how many times I've imagined you bent over with this perfect ass up in the air, you wouldn't argue."

She didn't, but he got an up close scent and view of her pussy moistening at his words. Not immune to compliments. Good to know.

When the water ran piping hot, he stepped into the shower with her still draped over his shoulder before he set her down, a slow, sensuous slide down his body that showed her just how much he liked her body. She peeked up at him through coyly fluttering lashes and smiled.

"I am really starting to like the way you think, shifter. Multi-tasking. Nice, *very* nice."

With a grin, he grabbed the soap and ran it over her luscious body, loving her hourglass curves. No skin and bones here. She was all woman. *My woman.*

The feel of her silky smooth skin as he ran his soapy hands over her made him harder than a rock. He stroked her full breasts, rolling her nipples until they hardened, then slid a hand between her thighs to stroke her slick folds.

Wet and ready for him already.

He dropped to his knees in the tub, his face inches from her curls. Hearing her gasp, he looked up and lust roared through him as he saw her gazing down at him, her green eyes glowing with desire.

"Lick me, Ryker."

He almost came at her bold, huskily murmured words, and his inner cat roared. "Oh, my little *heksen*, I am going to make you scream."

Spreading her willing thighs, he buried his face into the part of her that smelled so decadently woman—and delicious. Her plump lips parted before his tongue and fingers, her moist core tasting so sweet. He lapped at her, his mouth unerringly finding her clit and sucking it.

Caught up in the pleasure he lavished upon her, she didn't seem to note how hard she tugged his hair. Not that he cared about the pain, or the fact he could end up bald. He liked it when she got rough and wild. He gripped her plush ass cheeks to hold her steady as she gyrated and trembled under his oral assault. Tonguing her, he could feel her inner muscles starting to quiver and he knew she was ready to come for him. Both he and his cat growled in satisfaction—*mine*.

Ryker stood up and turned her around. He placed his hand in the middle of her back and pushed to bend her over. She complied, exposing her pink pussy to him and providing a target for his cock. So many times he'd imagined this moment; it didn't compare to the reality. He also couldn't stem his impatience. He drove into her welcoming wetness as she braced her hands on the shower wall and let out a cry, which turned into a scream of pleasure.

"That's it, little witch. Take it. Take all of me." And she

did, thrusting back against him, inviting him to go deeper, harder. Holy fuck, it was heaven.

Feeling himself approaching the brink much too fast and not wanting to crest alone, Ryker reached a hand forward and curved it under her body, finding her sweet spot. He rubbed with one calloused finger while vigorously pumping, the gripping feel of her pelvic muscles making him tremble. *I have to hold on until she comes first.* Thankfully, his stroking proved too much for her to handle. With another scream, she shattered around his cock, her slick muscles squeezing him tight.

Grabbing her waist with both of his hands, he pounded her, quick and pistonlike. Her soft backside fit perfectly into the hollow of his groin, a soft cushion for the pushing that made him lose control.

It did not escape him, even amidst the loss of his control, that she took what he gave and whimpered for more.

More? His sweet witch wanted more. *She is so fucking made for me.*

His beast mistook his mental euphoria as assent and took control. Long canines descended into his mouth. Before he could say bad kitty, he'd pulled her upper body partially up and leaning forward, he clamped his teeth down on the nape of her neck.

As he tasted the metallic fluid that signaled he'd broken her skin, she went rigid. With a long scream of his name, she came around his shaft a second time. A gushing, scalding wetness soaked his prick still buried balls deep inside her. He came wildly, his cock spurting jet after jet of cream. His whole body shuddered with the force of his release. Slowly, his mouth let go of her skin, the round mark of his teeth vivid on her previously unblemished flesh.

Oops.

He knew he should feel bad about marking, after all, he hadn't exactly asked her first. However, knowing the answer—No—he figured he'd explain what the mark meant later. Much, much later. Maybe after he'd gotten her drunk. Or had her handcuffed to something. It would suck if she killed him before realizing that being mated to him wasn't the end of the world.

In the meantime, until he got brave enough to tell her, he'd have to content himself with knowing she belonged to him, a fact that made his cat finally curl up with a satisfied purr to sleep.

As if the force of their coupling had taken their voices, he and his witch quietly finished washing. She stepped out and wrapped a fluffy towel around her body. Watching her walk out of the bathroom, he found himself stunned at the possessive—and scary—feelings he felt developing for her. *Feelings I'd better not mention to her or she'll just think of something insulting to say.*

She was so damned cute that way.

18

"If we've got to hit your place, then we're taking my car," Evangeline said, dangling some keys.

Ryker took in her appearance and apparently lost his voice because he kept staring, speechless. Judging by the bulge in his pants, Evangeline had achieved her desired look—pretty damned hot. Knowing her glamor would be useless around the vamps and Ryker, she'd dressed with care. Drawing attention to her lush curves, she elected to wear a long black skirt with slits on the sides that rose obscenely high on her thighs. A tight black corset constricted her breasts so much she appeared to have bottomless cleavage. Stiletto heels for extra height and darkly kholed eyes, teased curls, and bright red lips completed her look.

While she lied to herself and blamed her slutty preparation on their upcoming meeting with the blood suckers, Evangeline couldn't deny the girly part of her—that she wanted to strangle—also dressed for her feline lover. Would he notice? Appreciate? Admire?

She didn't quite hold her breath, but couldn't deny a certain amount of nervous anxiety. He didn't disappoint when he saw the end result. Eyes glinting gold, he watched her as a cat would a mouse—hungrily.

Of course, he didn't look as yummy wearing an old boyfriend's track pants and a t-shirt a few sizes too small. However, even dressed like an idiot, he exuded maleness.

"Stop that," he growled.

"What?" she purred back, her movements fluid and sensual as she sidled up to him.

"Looking at me like that."

"Like what?"

"Like a cougar on the prowl. You know, I can smell your arousal." He closed his eyes and clenched his fists at his side. "So sweet. Tempting."

Evangeline's eyelids grew heavy as her body flushed hotter with passion. Now that she'd let her libido run loose, it seemed foolish to deny or hide her desire for him. She ran a red-tipped finger down his chest. "Wanna taste? This skirt has easy access."

"Dammit, witch. You truly are wicked."

She didn't take offense at his words, not when she could see the tent in his pants, surely painful given the way the fabric confined his sizable girth.

While the role of seductress was new to her, she couldn't deny her enjoyment at his discomfort. A husky laugh burst free from her. "Poor kitty. I'll try and behave." She tossed him a naughty smile and added. "Maybe."

"You'll pay for your torture later."

"I should hope so. But enough bantering. Come, it's time we got you ready to play with some vamps." She strutted past him, only letting out a small squeal when his hand slapped her ass. Rubbing her stinging posterior, she flashed him a dirty look. He responded with an arrogant male grin.

As if she'd let that pass.

They almost didn't make it out the door. And she ended up having to fix her lipstick.

Arriving at her car, an older model four-door sedan, he insisted on driving and she let him. *I would never admit this aloud, but I could watch him all day.* Big or not, he handled himself with a self assured grace and restrained power that came from strength and cocky confidence. Attractive didn't come close to describing it.

But watching him wasn't the only reason she let him drive. He knew how to handle a motorized vehicle much better than she did. She preferred traveling by broom—or more recently, plastered to the back of a hunk on a bike. A hunk she'd just fucked. A hottie she planned to screw again. Maybe even in this car.

Her panties grew damp and he growled. "Stop that."

Evangeline chuckled. *Damn, I should have fucked him the first night we met. For the first time in a long time, I'll admit I'm having fun.* "Why?"

"Because if you don't, I'm gonna pull over and fuck you until the windows fog over and this car is rocking on its struts."

"Promises, promises."

"Evil witch."

"Naughty kitty. Tempting a poor girl then not following through."

"Think of it as foreplay for later."

"Who says there'll be a later?"

He shot her a look and she laughed. No use in denying when they both knew they'd enjoy several *laters*.

She behaved herself the rest of the way to his home, more or less. Crossing and uncrossing her legs. Letting her fingers dance on his muscled thigh. Giving him a hand job when they got on the highway, admonishing him to drive straight lest he kill them both.

What a fun road trip. They arrived at their destination intact. The large house with the hedged-in yard whose driveway he pulled into didn't surprise her, but the tiny woman who opened the front door as they walked up did.

Evangeline's nails dug into Ryker's arm, probably drawing blood. "Who is she?" Evangeline hissed, the green serpent of jealousy rising immediately to boil her blood.

The jerk smiled. "It's not what you think, my little witch. Ma, what are you doing here?"

Staring at the tiny woman who'd birthed the giant beside her, Evangeline hoped they'd given her lots of drugs, heavy duty ones, because that had to have hurt.

Casting a not so nice glare in Evangeline's direction, she said, "I was worried about you. Besides, isn't a mother allowed to visit her son?"

It seemed Evangeline wasn't the only one with a manipulative mother. She released Ryker's arm so he could enfold his mother in a big hug. After a bone-crushing embrace, he turned and gestured to Evangeline. "Ma, I'd like you to meet a friend of mine. This is Evangeline. Evangeline, my mother, Aneka."

Aneka smiled at her, but Evangeline noticed it didn't reach her eyes, but then again, neither did her own smile. "A pleasure to meet you, ma'am."

"Please, call me Aneka. Won't you come inside? I just made some coffee." Aneka turned and walked into the house as if she owned it, but Ryker made no move to follow.

"Fuck. Fuck. Fuck." He chanted the word as if it would help.

Judging by his annoyance, at least she knew he'd not planned this meeting. Evangeline nudged Ryker in the ribs and whispered up to him naughtily, "Yes, I'd like to, but it might be kind of weird with your mother inside."

Startled, he smiled down at her ruefully. "My mother being here is not good."

"Why? She doesn't look as if she could hurt a fly." Not because she seemed gentle tempered, more like she lacked the size to do any damage.

"My mother is much tougher than she looks. Just watch yourself around her. When she gets into one of her moods, she can be quite nasty."

Well, so can I. Although for the sake of the wicked sex with Ryker, she'd make an effort to be—*gag*—nice.

Bracing herself for the inevitable confrontation, Evangeline walked into the ring—er, house.

If she cared about other people, she might have paid attention to the interior of the house that screamed, "a man lives here," but since she highly doubted the wood paneled finishes and scratched hardwood floors had anything to do with his sexual prowess, she couldn't care less. Although, she did almost smile at the cute picture of him as a kid with no front teeth.

As if he knew exactly where she looked, he said over his shoulder, "That picture was taken after my first fight with a bear shifter at school. I raked in a ton of dough with the tooth fairy that night."

"I take it you won?"

Aneka's snort from ahead of them said it all.

As they entered a kitchen dressed in wooden cabinets and stainless steel appliances, Aneka immediately grabbed mugs from the cabinet and prepared coffee to go round.

Evangeline watched with entertainment as Ryker's mother tried very hard not to slam every item down on the counter. *Someone's in a mood and I'll bet I'm the cause. This is going to get interesting.*

Ryker's forehead creased as he watched his mother. She could see his hesitation at leaving them alone. But they needed to visit with the vampires and the clock was a ticking.

"You'd better get ready for our meeting," said Evangeline, capable of fighting her own battles. And looking forward to it. *Stubborn mother, prepare to meet a wicked witch.*

With a smile as false as her own, if with a lot more teeth, Aneka agreed. "Go, son. I'm sure your *friend* and I will get along wonderfully."

As if anybody believed that lie.

"No blood," he admonished as he walked out shaking his head. Oh how cute. He trusted her not to kill his mother. Idiot.

"All right, spit it out," said Evangeline, looking Aneka in the eye, not one to dance around. "You're obviously not happy about something and I'm guessing it has to do with Ryker."

"You will stay away from my son," warned Aneka, her eyes hard and uncompromising.

"Why would I do that?" asked Evangeline, perching herself on a stool.

"I can smell your filthy magic, witch. I will not have my boy tainted by your kind."

Evangeline rolled her eyes. "Oh, please. My magic doesn't work on him and you know it. Not to mention the whole interspecies thing means no babies. So why don't you just butt out? Ryker and I are just having fun while on a job. Big fucking deal."

"It is a big deal. I've got plans for Ryker."

"He's a big boy. Why don't we let him decide what he wants?"

"Because he's a man and men often think with the wrong body part."

"Lucky for you, I don't use him for thinking." With a slow lick of her lips, Evangeline made it obvious what she did use him for.

Aneka's eyes narrowed. "Filthy slut."

"Such language." Evangeline pretended shock before letting loose an evil chuckle. "Don't make me wash your mouth out with soap."

"Are you threatening me?"

"I'm sorry. Was I being too subtle? To clarify, yes. I am. I will fuck your son if and when I like, and if you continue to call me names, I will make you regret it whether you're his mommy or not."

"Witch, you don't know who you're messing with." Aneka's form wavered from petite woman to that of a large, striped cat with very, big teeth.

Oh, how juvenile. Evangeline yawned. "I really hope you've got more than that." Narrowing her own eyes, Evangeline smiled coldly even as she formed an invisible bubble around Aneka, careful to make sure the edges didn't touch the shape-shifter. Once formed, she sucked the air out of it. Evangeline almost giggled at the beauty of it. And to think it only took a single phone call, bitching to her grandfather about shape-shifters and their immunity to magic. *I love that Granddad taught me to think outside the box. Like using indirect magic against shifters, beautifully effective.*

Standing in front of the gasping woman, Evangeline shook her head in a chiding manner. "What's wrong? Cat got your tongue?" She grinned her nastiest smile. "Let's get one thing straight here. I actually kind of like your son. At least in the bedroom. I know, hard to believe. Trust me, I have a hard time believing it myself. While I like him, I can guarantee no one will hurt or fuck with him, or if they do, it won't be something they'll live to tell. Now, you might be his mommy, which means by default I have to keep you out of a coffin, but—" Evangeline leaned closer to the airless vacuum she'd created and met the bulging eyes of Ryker's mother. "You will not fuck with me or insult me. At least not to my face. Do we *understand* each other?"

A begrudging nod from Aneka and Evangeline dropped the bubble.

For a second, a gleam of admiration entered Aneka's eye. "It's a pity you weren't born a shifter."

"But then we wouldn't be having this wonderful time getting to know each other," said Evangeline sweetly as Ryker walked in holding a large studded collar.

A typical male, Ryker seemed oblivious to the undercurrents, which suited Evangeline just fine. After all, he might take offense with the knowledge Evangeline had kind of choked his mother.

"I see you both survived." He glanced around the pristine kitchen.

"Was there really any doubt? We had a lovely chat while you were gone."

Aneka snorted, but kept silent.

Ryker tossed them both a suspicious look, but chose not to ask. Smart man.

"What the hell is that for?" asked Evangeline, indicating the collar in his hands while at the same time wondering if it had matching cuffs. The things she could do with him spread eagle...

Dammit. Evangeline really needed to do something about the whole he-could-smell-her-arousal thing because Ryker growled softly, and with a squeak, Aneka said, "I think I'd better leave. Yes, I, um, need to go do something, elsewhere. Out of this house elsewhere."

Evangeline didn't even wave goodbye as Ryker's mother left. She only had eyes for the big man stalking toward her, his eyes wavering between his intense blue and the golden that indicated his reciprocal arousal.

"So who won the fight?" he asked.

Lips curling in a triumphant grin, Evangeline licked her lips at the naughty gleam in his eye. "The wickedest witch never loses. Would you believe we came to a mutual *understanding*?"

He let out a bark of laughter that turned into a strangled moan when she rubbed up against him and cupped his groin.

"Now that I've passed the mommy test, do I get a prize?"

"I swear, witch, after we're done with our meeting

with the vamps, I am going to pleasure you until you can't move."

"Promise?" she whispered.

His hard kiss left little doubt he meant what he said.

I can't wait.

19

As Ryker padded alongside Evangeline in the form of his beast—a large, black, deadly panther—he thought over her reaction to his change of form back at his place.

Slapping his studded leather collar on the counter, he'd outlined his plan to accompany her in his beast form.

"You want to go as my black cat? Sort of like a witch's familiar?" she'd said, tapping her chin back at his place. "I like it." Then she'd looked at him expectantly.

A part of him had wanted to shy from her keen eyes —*how will she react to my changing in front of her?* But his witch had guts. If any woman could handle the disturbing image of a man morphing into a beast, she could. Shedding his clothes, he stood in front of her naked and erect. He just couldn't help himself around her. With an ability only natural born alphas owned—the others able to only change during extreme emotions or a full moon—he'd coaxed his beast into taking over. It needed little urging. With a roar, the beast took over, his human form suddenly sprouting the fur, structure, and musculature of a jungle cat, all in the blink of an eye.

Evangeline said not a word during his transformation, but her green eyes had opened wide in her face. Then she'd smiled, a big, beautiful grin of admiration. "Fucking fantastic. Look at you. What a big, beautiful kitty you are." To the man's disgust, but the panther's glee, she'd proceeded to rub his head, especially around the ears, and soon had his beast purring in delight.

Trust his witch to treat a dangerous predator like an overgrown house pet.

Once again, she'd passed yet another test, proving once again just how rightly his beast had chosen. *My mate.* The words didn't seem so shocking anymore; on the contrary, a sense of rightness and possessiveness suffused them. *The only problem will be making her accept it. My lovemaking is one thing. Somehow, I don't think she'll handle the whole I'm yours-for-life issue as well.*

When she'd placed the big black collar around his neck, she'd giggled without reason. Studded with gems and metal, it served as a prop to make him look more imposing. Stroking him, she leaned down and murmured the reason for her mirth—and scent of arousal.

"You'll have to wear this for me sometime, naked of course."

Yup. Fucking perfect for him.

She drove them to the vampire lair in her car, an experience he never wanted to repeat. She truly lived up to her reputation as a menace to society in so many ways.

An hour's drive with traffic, a few broken speed laws, and just past twilight, they found themselves outside of the city and in front of the large mansion that housed the vamps for the area. Awash in lights, the house lit up the encroaching gloom while strange howls and gibbering laughter announced their presence.

The one problem with Ryker wearing his kitty form was his inability to speak to Evangeline. He had to trust—that word almost made him cough up a hairball—that she had a plan. If not, he'd have to let his feline play. Something that might happen anyway given vamps were notorious seducers, a thought that made his fur bristle. *Mine.*

Any vamp so much as laid a finger on her, and they'd end up minus a limb. Ryker didn't share well with others.

Evangeline strutted in her heels and slitted skirt —*mmm creamy white thighs*—up the steps to the double front door. Without an ounce of fear—on the contrary, he could smell the anticipation emanating from her—she banged the metal knocker in the shape of a demon's head.

The eyes of the carving opened, their ruby red glow baleful. Its metallic lips curved into a sardonic smile when it said, "What do ye want, witch?"

"I'm here to speak to the coven leader."

"Is he expecting you?" asked the demonic face.

"I swear, you are just as bad as the knocker at Rumpelstiltskin's house."

"We're cousins. Gotta problem with that, hag?"

Lips pursed, he could smell her irritation mounting. "Listen you hunk of junk. I knocked out of courtesy and now you're pissing me off. Let me in before I get *really* annoyed, you animated piece of scrap metal." She didn't raise her voice as she threatened, but the fact she would not hesitate to act came through loud and clear.

"There's no need to be nasty," sulked the doorknocker before the door swung open with a theatrical squeak.

"Come along, kitty," she said, and holding her head imperially high, she strode into the bloodsuckers' lair.

Damn, she's got guts. He thanked the fact his cat had control over its sexual urges because he knew if he'd seen her like this as a man, he would have pressed her up against the wall and kissed her breathless. Who would have thought a woman of power would have proven so sexy?

With her wiggle leading the way, Ryker followed behind her, all senses on high alert. His nose, keener in this form, scented the air and the flavors that imbued it. *Dust, decay, undead thing. Ooh, yummy, a bleeding living thing.* Nothing surprising for a house full of vamps.

Unerringly, his witch strode into the vacant-seeming mansion, her heels clacking on the marble entrance floor. She seemed to know where she wanted to go and never paused or slowed down her pace even as she approached a pair of closed wooden doors. With a fling of her hand and a rush of power he could feel along his heightened senses, she flung the portals open for their grand entrance.

The sudden stench of bloodsuckers wafted out and Ryker's beast bared its teeth. *Fuck me, there are a lot of them.* His witch seemed not to notice, though. She entered the ballroom with the grace and confidence of a queen, glancing neither left nor right at the ranks of undead that lined the walls. The sound of her heels echoed loudly as the congregation of vamps fell silent, their dark eyes following her path to the throne at the far end of the grand ballroom.

Head swinging from side to side, Ryker made sure his large canines were visible and menacing. He didn't like the fact that so many vampires were gathered. The reports he'd studied about the vampires had not mentioned that this coven had grown so large. *I'll have to let the shifter council know.* A culling was perhaps in order.

When Evangeline came to a stop in front the throne, the silence hung thick all around them. You could have heard a mouse fart.

Nobody spoke a word. The battle of wills had begun.

It didn't take long for discomfort to set in. For everyone but his witch. She stood there, still as a statue in bored indifference, waiting, her expression flat, her eyes cold.

Around them, Ryker heard the ruffle of fabric as those in attendance shifted, unsure and discomfited.

The vampire on his throne gave in. He straightened from his slouch with an expression of displeasure. Platinum-haired with pale aristocratic features that some might have called handsome, he surveyed them, or more specifically, Evangeline. Ryker definitely didn't appreciate the interest that lit his expression as he eyed her up and down, trying to rile her. Still, she didn't say a word.

And won the stalemate.

"Miss Rasputin, what a delight to finally meet you," said the vamp, speaking with only the faintest hint of an accent.

"Let's hope you still feel that way in a few minutes, Mr. Delacroix."

"Pierre, please. And may I call you Evangeline?" Pierre smiled at her winsomely.

"No, you may not. My name is Ms. Rasputin to you."

Her answer took the bloodsucker aback, but he recovered quickly and smiled again, showing off his small, pointed canines. *Bah, those aren't teeth. I should show him mine.* As if the mere thought summoned his attention, Pierre's dark eyes flicked over to Ryker in his feline form and he raised an aristocratic brow. "My, what a big pussy you have, Ms. Rasputin."

"You know what they say, the bigger the better."

Had Ryker been in human form, he would have probably choked with laughter. His beast chuffed in amusement, especially at the uncertain look on the vamp's face. Unsettled, he didn't reply, but his eyes began to swirl and Ryker finally growled. *The fucker is trying to mesmerize her.*

He should try and remember to give his witch more credit.

Evangeline's laughter rang out. "Oh, Pierre, you really are new, aren't you? Did no one warn you that your mind tricks won't work on me? My grandfather taught me well." Her voice turned hard and the air grew thick as she drew power into herself. The static around her lifted her hair to dance wildly. "I am already tired of your games. I am on a schedule and have no time to waste playing. You will answer a few questions, truthfully of course, and then my cat and I will be on our way. Don't answer and you will annoy me. You *really* don't want to do that."

Pierre's pale face clenched with anger. "You presume much, witch. Even if my mind tricks don't work, I do happen to outnumber you."

Evangeline made a show of glancing around, her disdain so beautifully expressed on her face. "Yes, I see you've got visitors because we both know your coven is rather small compared to others. But, I know something you don't," she said, turning back to Pierre with a smirk.

The power she held made her eyes glow blacker than the vamp's.

"Really, and what would that be?" said the head vamp with more confidence now that he'd found his balls again in the realization he held the numbers.

"None of these sycophants will come to your aid when I rip your tongue out and shove it down your throat and make you cry for your maker."

He couldn't stop his surprised cough at her temerity, but Ryker managed to restrain himself from shaking his head at her outrageous threat. His witch certainly hadn't learned diplomacy growing up, but personally, he liked her style. Why screw around when threats and intimidation tended to work faster—not to mention provided more entertainment?

It seemed the bloodsucker didn't appreciate her unique qualities as much as Ryker did.

"Insolent bitch. Bring me her heart!" screamed Pierre. Four vamps behind the throne moved forward at his words and then halted indecisively. The undead lining the walls of the room watched the unfolding action with interest, but not one moved to do Pierre's bidding.

Evangeline chuckled and a wind whipped through the room, a cold breeze of power that swirled around her in a wild dance, showcasing who held its reins.

Standing up from his throne, Pierre glared out at his court. "Why do none of you obey? I gave an order."

A vampire with parchment thin skin that indicated his advanced age shook his head and answered. "I've lived this long for a reason. By being smart. I for one will not start a war with the Rasputin family. I would suggest you just answer the witch's questions."

Pierre did not heed the words of the elder bloodsucker and Ryker almost snorted in disbelief because he could see by the tautness of Pierre's body language he had no intention of backing down.

Fine with me. My beast could use a light workout.

20

EVANGELINE ALMOST LAUGHED WHEN PIERRE STUPIDLY gestured for his bodyguards to attack her, the only creatures in this room loyal enough to heed their master. Before she could take care of them, though, her big black panther dove forth with sharp, glistening canines.

My, what big teeth he has. Having never had someone come to her aid before, Evangeline stood back and decided to enjoy the show. She could always step in if he needed help. However, Ryker didn't disappoint.

With a savage snarl, Ryker sprang at the vamp nearest her and knocked it flat. Large claws on massive paws dug into the downed dead one and his big head swung left and right, quickly gauging the position of the other three. The vamps circled the black cat and their fallen comrade, hissing with their tiny pointed teeth.

Evangeline giggled. After all, did they really think those puny incisors would intimidate *her* big kitty? Ryker with a quick slice across the throat of the vamp he stood on—*ruthless, I like that*—coiled his powerful hind legs and jumped at his next victim. Chomp. Another vampire went down.

Ryker's tail swished from side to side in excitement as he contemplated the next in line. With a cry of, "Fuck this," the last two bloodsuckers fled.

Done playing, Ryker padded back to sit at Evangeline's side, and calmly licked his chops. Evangeline couldn't stop an odd warmth at his actions from spreading throughout her body and usually unresponsive heart. How could she not admire him? He not only came to her defense, he displayed the same feline grace and power while in his beast form that she so enjoyed of him when he was a man. She'd have to show him how much she liked it later. Time to conclude their business.

With a broad smile for Pierre, who had watched in morbid fascination, Evangeline reached down—not far because damn was his beast huge—and scratched the fur behind Ryker's ears. "Good kitty."

A rumbling purr that closely resembled the motor on a '67 Chevy startled her, but she managed to hide her reaction.

Pierre didn't and visibly flinched. If it was possible for a vampire to turn whiter than usual, then he did, which widened Evangeline's grin.

"Are we willing to be more amenable now, Pierre?" she asked sweetly.

"Ask your questions and be gone," Pierre said, his cocky airs gone.

"What is your involvement in the plan to kidnap Rumpelstiltskin's daughter?"

"None."

Evangeline noticed the flicker in his eyes. "You lie," she stated calmly. "I don't like liars."

When Pierre opened his mouth as if he would retort, Ryker growled and stood, the fur on his back bristling.

Swallowing, Pierre couldn't take his eyes from the panther, but he answered. "We are not involved, but we were approached."

"By whom?"

"We asked, but the messenger we were sent was under a mind compulsion and could tell us nothing about who had sent him."

"Where is this messenger? I'd like to speak to him."

Pierre's lips curved into a smile. "We ate him."

"You're very lucky you didn't get food poisoning," she said, wiping the smile off Pierre's face. "It's what I would have done. So what did this messenger ask you? I want to hear the request word for word."

"He didn't say much. Just showed up at our door a few nights ago and asked to speak with the head vampire. We made him wait for a while before letting him in to talk with me. His exact words were, 'Kidnap the trickster's daughter and gain a boon for your coven.' I said, 'Not fucking likely,' and after that, not a word did the man speak. I admit we found this most disconcerting when we ate him for we are used to the screams of our victims."

"Didn't he have an ID on him? What did he drive?" These continual dead ends on the case were really starting to piss her off.

"A taxi dropped him off and he wore nothing on him—no wallet, identification, nothing to indicate whom he worked for."

"Well this was a complete waste of my time," she grumbled, turning on her heel. Without a goodbye or a glance at the vampires who eyed her exit with interest, she clacked her way to the front hall, her big, black kitty at her heels. She strode from the undead lair, pausing only for a moment when she hit the rich scent of the night. She closed her eyes for a second and breathed deep. *Disgusting creatures. And to think humans find them appealing.*

Personally, she found herself preferring the vitality and strength of a beast. Well, not just any beast—Ryker.

Opening the passenger door so he could leap in, she clambered into the driver's side and slammed the car into gear, annoyed at the time they'd wasted coming here. She'd only driven a small ways from the house when with barely a shiver, Ryker reverted back to his male self. Make that his very male and naked self.

Swerving back onto the road, she averted her eyes to the blacktop in front of her. *Apparently, I still haven't lost my fascination with his body.* A body whose nude flesh sat temptingly close.

"Pull over," he growled when the car lurched yet again.

Not bothering to argue, because truly, driving was not her forte, she pulled over onto the side of the road. But instead of opening her car door, she gave into desire. Turning sideways, she grabbed his face and kissed him, her hot tongue licking the seam of his lips and parting them to duel with his waiting organ. Eagerly, his hands pulled her onto his lap, the hardness of his erection poking her bottom.

They kissed fiercely, their hands grasping and rubbing the parts they could reach in their sitting position.

"Straddle me," he whispered.

Thanking the slits on her skirt and the wide seats in her car, Evangeline turned on his lap and placed her knees on either side of his thighs. Her moist core, covered only in a thin scrap of silk, rubbed against his throbbing cock.

"*Good*, little witch. You're ready for me, I see." With rough fingers, he tore the panties from her, placing her aching sex directly against his shaft. He reached down and with a thumb, stroked her clit, making her go wet and wild with need.

"Fuck me," she moaned.

She liked that he didn't make her ask twice. He simply lifted her high enough to sheathe his prick inside her, its hard length filling her up, deeper and deeper. *It is all about the size,* she thought, sighing at the feel of him stretching her.

With his hands on her waist and her fingers digging into his shoulders, she rode his cock, the close confines of the car making it tight but exciting. The sound of slapping flesh and panting breaths filled the car, the shocks of the vehicle absorbing some of the impact.

When his mouth licked hotly at her neck and bit her gently, pinching the skin, she screamed. Her orgasm hit her fast and hard, a pleasurable explosion that left her dizzy and soft in his arms. As if her orgasm was the catalyst he'd waited for, she felt him come inside her.

They sat there regaining their breath, his arms wrapped around her body, when she felt his lips brushing the top of her head and temple, so gentle and caring. She liked it enough she didn't push him away. *What is happening to me? Since when do I cuddle after sex?*

And why does it feel so right?

* * *

Ryker held in a sigh, not surprised when Evangeline scrambled off him. Her prickly exterior made it predictable even. What had surprised him was her diving on him all hot and horny like that in the first place. Mind you, he'd quite enjoyed it. Judging by her swollen lips, and her attitude, so had she and it didn't please her one bit.

My little heksen *doesn't like feeling dependent on anyone.*

Ryker grabbed his clothes off the back seat and got out of the car to dress. By the time he got around to the other side and opened the door to get in, she'd already scooted over to the passenger side, her face turned out the side window in an attempt to ignore him.

Not bloody likely.

Throwing the car into drive, he spun the tires on the gravel and shot out onto the road. Once they were on their way back to his place, he laid a heavy hand on her thigh and squeezed it.

"You did well back there," he said.

"Thank you," she replied, then to his shock, she laid her hand on top of his. "Your beast put on quite the show."

His kitty chuffed in his mind. "He was trying to impress you."

"Oh, he did."

Ryker squeezed her leg through the material of her skirt. The hand she'd rested on top grabbed his hand and lifted it. He expected her to fling it off, but instead, she pulled her skirt aside and placed his hand on the bare skin of her thigh. Startled, he looked over at her.

"I might not like you, shifter, but I won't deny you're a fantastic fuck."

With those romantic words, the car got pulled over again, and placing her outside on the hood of the car for more room, first he licked her until she cried out his name, then he fucked her until she called him her god.

Mine, oh mine, he thought possessively.

21

EVANGELINE WOKE IN A STRANGE BED, ALONE. SITTING UP, grabbing at the dark blue sheet, and holding it up to her chest, she peered around. Decorated in earth tones, the room screamed man cave from the blocky wooden furniture to the plaid comforter—not to mention the big ass TV on the wall at the foot of the bed.

Ryker's room. She vaguely remembered coming back here last night. She'd fallen asleep in the car, a fact that surprised her as she never slept around people. It made her too vulnerable. Yet sleep in Ryker's presence she had, and she didn't even protest when he carried her to bed, stripped her, tucked her in, and then cuddled her.

Evangeline lay back on the bed and groaned. *Oh my God, we slept together, spooning like a couple.* It might sound odd, but with all the boyfriends she'd had—most short lived—she'd never spent the night, well, not asleep anyway, and she definitely never snuggled. She tended to be a let's-fuck-and-leave kind of gal.

However, Ryker kept making her break all kinds of

rules. *At least I'm not in love and neither is he. This is just good sex. Make that fucking fantastic sex. Nothing more.*

She certainly didn't feel warm and mushy feelings inside when she read the note on the pillow beside her saying he'd gone to get coffee and doughnuts. Nope, that giddy feeling inside? Just hunger.

His bedroom had a bathroom attached to it, and she quickly showered the scent of sex off her skin. Her mind drifted as she bathed, imagining him joining her slick and naked in the shower, his big hands roaming, soaping her up and... Ack! Out she jumped, barely rinsed. Grabbing a towel, she scrubbed herself dry with more vigor than needed, trying to dispel the erotic spell she almost put herself under. She refused to moon over him. *I am not some love-struck idiot.* And she needed to stop acting like one.

With her hair wrapped atop her head in a towel and wearing an oversized t-shirt of Ryker's—which smelled uniquely of him—she wandered out into his home, not realizing she had company until she walked into the kitchen and ran into his mother.

"Are you still here?" asked Evangeline, not even bothering to couch her query in politeness as she perched on a stool. "Don't you have better things to do like chase some rats in a sewer? Or climb up a tree?"

"Aren't you just a ray of sunshine in the morning. And to think I was going to buy you a new broom so you could fly your fat ass out of here."

Fat? "Your son wasn't complaining about the size of my bottom last night. On the contrary, he complimented, *several times.*"

The sprayed coffee as Aneka choked made her smile. "Ever hear of too much information?"

"Ever hear of cutting the apron strings?"

"You won't get rid of me so easily, witch. I'm here to make sure Ryker doesn't do anything stupid," said Aneka.

"Stupid? Like visiting a vampire coven with me last night? I never saw a kitty have so much fun playing with dead things." Evangeline smirked at the pinched expression on Aneka's face.

"Ryker can take care of himself."

"So I saw last night. He was also very good about taking care of me." And she didn't mean just the sex.

"I don't care if he beds you. He's slept with his share of sluts over the years. But if you think I'm going to let him take you as his mate…"

Whoa. Why would his mother even raise that as a possibility? Theirs was a temporary arrangement. "Mate? Never. You don't have to worry on that account. I have no intention of getting hitched with anyone, least of all a shifter."

"Good. I have bigger plans for my boy. His bride has already been chosen for him. A nice shifter girl who is waiting for him to come home so they can get married."

A sudden fury, hinging on an inexplicable jealousy, consumed her. *A bride? For Ryker? Over my dead fucking body.* Evangeline almost said those words out loud. *No, wait a second. Why do I care? He's just a fuck friend. Nothing more.*

Her rationale did nothing to calm the anger simmering under her skin, not that she let it show. "Don't worry, once my sister's wedding and this job are done, we'll have no reason to see each other." Or keep him alive. Jerk. Annoyed at the thought of Ryker with another woman—and of never seeing him again—Evangeline pivoted on the stool lest she betray her jealousy to the other woman.

"What the hell is that on your neck?" Aneka spoke in a low, furiously cold tone.

Reaching with her fingers to touch her nape, Evangeline encountered the indents of the bite mark Ryker had left when they'd fucked so gloriously in the shower at her place the day before. The man's passion and stamina knew no bounds. She'd miss that about him.

"It's a love bite. Haven't you ever seen one?"

Aneka laughed nastily. "You fool. Shifters only bite for one reason. Or didn't you do any homework on our kind? He's marked you as his mate."

With a sinking feeling she'd not often experienced in her life, Evangeline turned to face Ryker's mother. "Excuse me? Say that again."

"You, my dear witch, are for all intents and purpose, married to my son. Don't you know anything? I guess not judging by the look on your face." Aneka shook her head while Evangeline absorbed the shocking news. "See, when a shifter finds his mate, while in the throes of sex, he bites her, hard enough to break skin and leave a lasting scar. In this way, he marks her as his. Think of it as a permanent tattoo that announces to all that you are no longer available. Congratulations, like it or not, you belong to Ryker. Welcome to the family." Aneka said the last with a bitter laugh that left no doubt as to the truth of her words.

A surge of warmth enveloped Evangeline—*he chose me as his mate!*—quickly followed by rage. *That fucker. He had no right.*

"How do we undo it?" Evangeline asked.

"You can't, *daughter*."

"Don't call me that."

"Why not? You're family now. Better get used to it. Wait until I tell the rest of the pride."

"No. I refuse to accept it. There has to be a way to reverse it."

"Yeah. Death."

She arched a brow. "Is that all? I am going to fucking kill him," Evangeline muttered darkly.

"Kill who?" asked the object of her ire, striding into the kitchen, looking much too delicious.

"You dirty, rotten bastard!" Evangeline screeched, jumping up from the stool. "How dare you make me your mate?"

"Who told you that?"

Aneka cleared her throat.

He shot a dark look at his mother. "Ma!"

"Not my fault you didn't tell her what the bite meant first. I saw it and remarked on it."

"You should have kept your mouth shut."

"Don't you yell at your mother. How fucking dare you claim me without permission, you animal." With a tug on her magic, Evangeline encased him in a bubble, like she had his mother previously, and sucked the air out. He, however, didn't panic. Ryker took a step forward and shattered the bubble, her magic evaporating when it came in contact with his body. Stupid bastard had figured out the loophole in her trick.

"I didn't do it on purpose or willingly," he shouted back.

Surely his words hadn't caused the stab of pain that

arced through her heart? "Oh gee. That makes it all better. You accidentally bit me and made me your wife."

"I couldn't help myself."

"And that's supposed to make it alright?"

"I was going to tell you."

"Too late."

"Now that you know, can't we talk about it? I know it's not what you expected. What either of us expected."

"You think? I am not discussing this. As a matter of fact, I'm leaving."

"You can't leave. We're bound for life."

"That's what you think. Goodbye, Ryker. Have a good life, asshole, alone, because I am not going to be a part of it." Nor would his last very long. First chance she got, after the wedding, she was going to annihilate his much too sexy ass.

Swiping her car keys from his hand as she dashed past, she tried to evade the hands that reached to grab, but again, his size won. Bands of steel wrapped around her and he turned her to face him.

"Stop it, Evangeline. What's done is done."

Done by accident. He didn't want me. No one ever wants me.

Moisture pooled in her eyes, and aghast that she might actually start to cry in front of him, she did the only thing she could think of to get him to let her go.

She kissed him.

22

THE BRIMMING MOISTURE IN HER EYES MADE RYKER'S HEART ache and his beast pace. He knew she didn't yet have the same strong feelings for him that he bore for her, but why the tears? Surely she didn't find him so horrible?

Apparently not because she kissed him. Her lips, so soft against his, trembled, and sensing her vulnerability, he loosened his grip on her and set her feet back on the floor. *She just needs time to get used to the idea.* The shock of finding out he'd claimed her took her by surprise. Once she took a bit of time to reflect on it, she'd realize it wasn't so bad. They were well suited, after a fashion. They certainly got along well in the bedroom; as for outside the bedroom, they made a good team as well. She'd see, they could—

The sudden pain on his instep as she stomped, followed by the excruciating agony in his groin as she kneed him hard, made him instinctively hunch over. It also sucked all coherent thought out of his head. Even amidst his suffering, though, he heard the slamming of the front door and the gunning of the car.

Fuck. She left. Left before he could make things right.

Wheezing and hoping she hadn't done permanent damage to his man parts—he'd need them for later when he caught up to Evangeline—he faced his mother with a glare. This was all her fault.

"You just *had* to tell her, didn't you?"

"What I'd like to know is why you didn't tell me? I'm your mother."

Ryker pinched the bridge of his nose and admonished his pacing beast to settle down. Much as his mother drove him insane, he still couldn't eat her. "I didn't admit what I did to you, or her, because I was waiting for the right moment. *Say in a few years when she wouldn't have freaked!*" He shouted the last, annoyed with his mother, but even more annoyed with himself. *Did Evangeline leave crying because she's confused and has feelings or does she truly hate me and never want to see me again?*

"You care for her, don't you?" said his mother quietly.

Incredulous, he stared at her. "Of course I do. She's my mate."

"Your animal is one thing. I'm talking about *you*, the man. You feel for her."

Ryker didn't even need to think about it before replying. "Yes, I care for her. A lot. She's not scared of me, Ma. Do you know how great that feels to not have her cower? When I get all big and bad, she smiles. She treats my beast like a giant kitty. She's fearless and beautiful. Sexy, smart, ruthless, and..."

"Holy fuck. You love her."

Like her? Yes. But love her? Ryker shook his head. "No.

I can't. It's too soon. Hell, she doesn't even like me most of the time."

"And?"

"What do you mean and? Love takes time. Trust. We have none of those things."

"Really? And is that all you think love is based on?" asked his mother with a wry smile. "Here's a question for you? Has she left your thoughts since you met?"

He shook his head.

"How do you feel about never seeing her again?"

His stomach clenched.

"What will you do if she finds another man?"

The roar that burst forth shocked him, but not his mother.

"You big, dumb idiot. You love her."

"And she hates me."

"Maybe not. Go after her. Talk to her."

"But she's pissed." And liable to try and kill him. Not exactly a great way to start their mated life together.

"She's scared because her feelings are frightening her. I don't think your witch handles emotions well. She's used to being a loner. Just like someone else I know. Show her you care. Make her listen. And good luck."

Incredible. Advice from his mother on how to keep his witch. Ryker cocked his head and looked at her. "Are you sure you're okay, Ma? You do remember she's a witch, right? Yet here you are telling me to go after her. Shouldn't you be freaking right about now and going after her ready to rip her head off?"

"Yeah, it's a shame about her sorceress blood. She'd have made a great shifter. But, even I can't fight fate or decide who you'll love. I might be bossy, but only because

I care for you, Ryker. If she makes you happy, then I'll just have to learn to live with it. Now go, quickly, before she does something stupid."

Ryker didn't wait any longer, almost running for the front door and his bike parked in the driveway. But he could have sworn he heard his mother say behind him, almost ruefully, "What a pity they can't conceive together. The babies they would have made."

23

THE POUNDING ON HER DOOR WOULDN'T LET UP, BUT Evangeline refused to give in.

"Come on, Evangeline. Can't we talk about this? It's not that bad."

"Oh yeah, what does your fiancée think about you accidentally marrying a witch?" Oh how Evangeline longed to scalp the unknown woman.

"I don't have a fiancée," he said with a heavy sigh.

"Not according to your mother."

"I can explain if you'd just open this damned door," he yelled.

"Bullshit. Try explaining how you claimed me as your mate without my permission," she shouted back. *He didn't mark me because he loves me.* And why that should matter she couldn't have explained, but it did.

Rotten fucking shifter. Marking me like some kind of possession. How barbaric—and hot. Evangeline hated the warmth that coiled though her at the thought of being *his*. She didn't need a man. She belonged to herself. So why, oh why, did an annoying girlie part of her long to throw open the door?

She knew the sex would be incredible. Make that mind-blowing, especially in their current moods. He'd ride her hard, his thick muscles straining and slick with sweat. Evangeline couldn't help the wetness that pooled between her legs, but still she wouldn't give in.

The pounding paused for a minute and in the silence, she could have sworn she heard sniffing. "Open this damn door, witch," Ryker roared. "I can smell you, and you can't deny it. You want me."

Evangeline, though, had stubbornness in droves and, crossing her arms over her chest, she stuck her tongue out at the door in a childish gesture he couldn't see but she personally enjoyed.

Crack!

The doorjamb splintered. The door swung open and, with a heavy thump, hit the wall.

Six-foot-something of bristling shifter stalked in with glowing golden eyes and the muscles in his torso bulging with tension. Evangeline couldn't help the jolt of desire that struck like lightning between her thighs and the heaviness that overtook her breasts.

Ryker bore a wild look about him, barely in control, a man pushed beyond the edge of reason. "Dammit, Evangeline. Why do you have to be so bloody stubborn? I want you to let me explain, but if you don't stop looking at me like that, I'm not going to be able to control myself. You drive me fucking wild."

Her tongue darted out and licked her lips, a motion he caught, and with a groan of need, he crushed her to his chest.

"My little *heksen*," he murmured.

His lips plundered hers, taking and drinking deeply of her like a man parched in the desert. She understood the feeling, because she thirsted for him too. She soaked in his kiss and opened her mouth wider for more, her limbs wrapping around him sinuously, holding him tight to her body.

Deny it all she wanted. Hate him as well. But when it came to passion, she couldn't help herself.

He kicked the splintered door shut behind them, and she absently wove some magic to keep it shut before he carried her to the bedroom and crawled onto the bed with her clinging to him. She knew she should send him away, but her hormones had taken over and they didn't want to think beyond the pleasure.

Her hands were taken from around his neck and pinned above her head by his in a gesture of dominance that made her gasp. His heavy weight nestled between her thighs and pinned her. Evangeline squirmed and panted. This submissive feeling was new and surprisingly exciting.

Using his lips and teeth, he tugged at the fabric of her shirt; his shirt actually, since she hadn't had the time—or heart—to change out of it when she got home.

Baring her breasts, he blew on her nipples until they stood erect and begged for attention.

"I'm going to tell you a story, my sweet *heksen*."

"Can't it wait?" she groaned, arching her breasts up to his mouth, which hovered out of reach.

Bending his head, Ryker bit down on a nipple, making her twitch and cry out.

"Quiet, my wild *heksen*, and listen."

"Why do you keep calling me *heksen*?" she asked.

"It's Danish for witch. Think of it as a term of endearment."

"Oh." She'd never had a lover give her a nickname before. Although, most of her enemies had; the most common term rhymed with witch.

"Are you ready to listen?"

"I'd rather you did other things with your mouth," Evangeline replied with a pout.

His tongue laved her nipple, a liquid line of fire that shot right to her groin. "Be a good little witch and you will be rewarded."

"If this is about the mating thing—"

His lips cut off her protest. "Enough," he said, his breathing erratic when he came up for air. "Now pay attention. Not too many people know this story, but I'm going to tell you since my mother obviously left out a lot of details when she claimed I was engaged. Vivian, my *ex*-fiancée," he stressed, "was the daughter of my mom's best friend and our next door neighbor. My mom originally wanted her to marry my older brother, but the age gap of fifteen years was a bit much, so they decided I should be the one instead to join our families."

"And I care because?" Evangeline said sarcastically, already hating this Vivian person.

"Because you are obviously jealous and yet have no need."

"I am not jealous."

"Liar." He sucked her breast into his mouth and she writhed under him. "Like I was saying, our mothers arranged a marriage between me and Vivian."

Realizing he would just keep torturing her if she didn't

listen, she decided to pay attention—for the moment. And being the multi-tasking type, she started thinking up ways of hurting the girl next door, Vivian. Very painful ways.

* * *

"Are arranged marriages common for your kind?" Evangeline asked, seeming resigned to listen.

Ryker almost breathed a sigh of relief when she seemed agreeable to hearing his tale even as he grimaced at her question. "Unfortunately, yes."

Evangeline let out a throaty laugh that made him grind his hips against hers, cutting her laugh short and turning it into a moan. "Oh, how barbaric," she said breathily.

"I wouldn't talk. I've heard about your virgin witch and Satan ritual. Isn't that how your sister met her fiancé?"

Evangeline didn't have to answer because the blooming color in her cheeks said it all. "Touché. So, you were betrothed against your will. What happened next?" she asked.

"Yes, well, being almost seven years older than Vivian, we didn't really see each other much when she was young. When she did start going to the same school, I was grades ahead of her, not to mention I dropped out at fifteen."

"Couldn't control the beast and your hormones at the same time?"

At least she hadn't assumed he was an idiot, but had instead jumped to the correct conclusion. "Exactly. As you know, keeping humans ignorant is the number one motto. When I really started noticing girls, so did my beast, and let's just say he really wanted to come out and play. I didn't see Vivian much for the next couple of years, and then I moved to the city for work and only went home for holidays. I'd actually pretty much forgotten about her until she turned eighteen and my mom started bugging me to come home and meet her."

Seeing his witch's eyes darken, Ryker dipped his head and circled both her nipples, one at a time, with his tongue, until she softened and sighed. Then he continued. "I put it off for over two years, but then my father spoke up, and no one says no to the alpha of the pack."

"That must have stuck in your craw, taking orders from someone, even your own dad."

Again, she'd struck the nail on the head. "Noticed my stubborn tendencies, did you? Well, being a good son, I went back prepared to do my duty to my clan. I shouldn't have bothered. Vivian was a pussy, literally. She fainted the first time she saw me."

"I know you're good-looking, but really, that's taking it far."

The surge of emotion that surged through him at her innocently spoken words took him by surprise and his beast growled softly—*mine*. Ryker's lips claimed hers in a heated kiss that left them panting.

"She didn't faint because I am God's gift to women. She passed out 'cause supposedly, I scared her."

"Stupid bitch."

Evangeline's heated words warmed him—and from a woman who professed to not care for him. They also dissipated the remaining anger, and yes, shame, he'd felt over Vivian's reaction. Never mind the other women who had always dropped their panties if he smiled at them, the fact that Vivian had reacted that way had humiliated, and surprisingly enough, hurt him. But still, he'd tried to do his duty by his clan.

"Even given her apparent fear and dislike for me, our families forged ahead with the wedding plans."

"You would have been miserable. Why did no one stop it?" Her green eyes looked up at him and he could see the ire in them, but not directed at him. No, she was angry for him. How strange it felt to have someone on his side, but he also liked it, liked it a lot.

"They thought she'd get over her fear of me, and as my father told me, so long as I got babes on her, I could always get my pleasure elsewhere."

The look in Evangeline's eyes turned dark and dangerous. "Keep in mind, so long as you are in my bed, you will touch no other. I don't share," she threatened. Then as if realizing she'd admitted to wanting him still in her bed, she added quickly, "Not that we'll be together that much longer."

He bit back a smile. Under the lobe of her ear, his warm breath making her shiver, he purred. "Just so you know, if a man so much as lays a hand on you, I will rip him apart, then eat him—and I mean that quite literally."

Her entire body shuddered under his. "You say the hottest things. And speaking of eating, perhaps you could demonstrate that for me later, or better yet, now."

That comment almost made him come. His cock jerked like a caged beast in his pants and his inner cat roared—*Take her*! But, he needed to finish his story and get to the point he wanted to make.

"A week before the wedding, I got tired of her tears and avoidance, so I decided to confront her." What a mistake that turned out to be—and a blessing in disguise.

"She told me I disgusted her and that the very thought of me touching her made her ill. As far as she was concerned, I was a savage beast and if she had her way, she'd never marry me in a million years. After hearing that, I couldn't go through with it. I have my pride. So I walked." And the shit had hit the fucking fan.

He and his father were currently not on speaking terms, and his mother kept trying to make excuses for Vivian. However, since meeting Evangeline, Ryker had learned one very important thing. He and Vivian would never have worked even had he not scared her. His reaction, and that of his beast, made it clear. Only one woman could ever satisfy him—Evangeline. He loved everything about her from her feisty attitude to her cute, little nose. He even loved the way she showed no fear and gave as good as she got. Of course, he still had to convince her she felt the same way. She seemed to have a distinct aversion to relationships, and shifters in general.

"So what does this broken engagement have to do with us? I mean me?" she asked, averting her eyes, feigning indifference. The rapid beat of her heart gave her away.

"Did my mother explain to you how our beasts sometimes recognize their mates? The need to claim her and mark her as our own?"

"Kind of. Thanks for reminding me, asshole. Get off." She bucked under him like a wild cat. Ryker wondered if he should tell her he liked it. If he did, though, she'd probably stop.

His attempt to kiss her into submission met with nipping teeth. The metallic taste of blood in his mouth did not deter him. She'd earned the right to her anger. He had marked her without permission, never mind that he didn't regret it. At least he had the satisfaction of knowing no other male would or could claim her. Not if they wanted to live.

With her hands held tightly above her head, he tortured her breasts, having noticed their sensitivity. His lips caught one bud tightly and he rolled it, abrading the sensitive nub against his teeth. He opened his mouth wide and took her tit in his mouth, sucking on her and gradually feeling her tense, fighting motions relax as he continued his ministrations. Evangeline moved against him, her hips arching.

At the sound of a moan, he stopped his delicious calming measures.

"As I was saying..." She tensed slightly beneath him. He looked into her heavy-lidded eyes and saw her watching him warily. "My beast has never wanted to mark a woman until it met you."

"Not even Vivian?" She spoke tentatively and then seemed surprised at her question.

"Only you. I admit, I never expected my beast would react so strongly when it found our mate. Nor was I prepared for how overwhelming the need would be to claim you when we came together that first time."

"So you didn't actually want me?" Her voice seemed oddly subdued and he wanted to gnash his teeth. *I'm saying this all wrong, dammit.*

He rubbed his hardness against her. "Does that feel like I don't want you?"

"So, it's just sex?"

Ryker didn't know what to answer. He wanted to scream, "No, I fucking love you, you stubborn twit," but his mother's warning about Evangeline being scared of her feelings for him tempered his response. "I think we both can't deny that our bodies are in complete harmony. Maybe when we get to know each other better, something else will develop."

She gnawed her lip. "What does being your mate mean then, other than fucking a lot?"

Ryker controlled his surprise at how her question seemed accepting of the situation. "We are exclusive to each other. I touch and desire no one else and neither do you." Or else he and his beast would tear the other man to pieces.

"I can handle that. I am not moving in with you though," she scowled.

Yet, thought Ryker. If she thought she'd be sleeping alone ever again, then he'd soon disabuse her of that notion. "Fine. Anything else you want to ask?"

He could still see a hint of disappointment in her eyes, but he couldn't figure out what he'd done wrong. She'd stopped fighting him. She'd accepted their mated state, more or less. What had he forgotten?

"Am I going to turn furry on the full moon now that you've bitten me?"

Ryker roared with laughter. "Sorry, my sweet *heksen*. You're still one hundred percent witch. Contrary to popular belief, shifters are born, not created. Any other questions?"

"Yeah, when are you going to shut the fuck up and take care of your mate? You've tortured my body enough, don't you think?"

Ryker got the hint and set himself to the task of pleasing his mate.

* * *

Why aren't I killing him?

He'd admitted to marking her because he'd lost control. But he didn't love her. Although, he did imply something could grow given they already enjoyed an unhealthy—yet pleasurable—obsession with each other's bodies. *Why do I feel sad it's just about good sex? It's what I wanted, right? I mean it's not as if I wanted him to profess love for me or something. I'm a witch, and an evil one to boot. Who'd be stupid enough to fall in love with me?*

Pathetic. Just pathetic. So what did she do instead of reaching for a knife to slit his throat? She let him believe they could try and work at the whole mated thing. And maybe, a teensy tiny part of her allowed itself to hope that one day, he could feel something for her, something like her sister had with Christopher.

Closing her eyes and letting the sensual feel of his tongue and hands caress her body, so sweetly and reverently, she could almost pretend this shifter, this man she'd fought so hard against, did love her. When his cock slid into her wet pussy and his eyes caught hers, she could almost fool herself into thinking the soft, yet possessive look in his eyes might mean something.

Her climax claimed her fast and hard and he quickly followed suit, bellowing her name before going rigid above her. Rolling so he lay on his back with her sprawled on top of him, he stroked the tendrils of hair from her face. For a moment, he seemed on the verge of saying something, but he clamped his lips tight.

Disappointment tried to worm its way through her.

She bitch-slapped it back behind her stubborn wall of indifference.

"What now?" she asked.

"I wish we could lie in bed, screwing all day, but your sister's wedding is tomorrow and we still have no idea what's going on with Rumpelstiltskin's daughter."

Evangeline frowned. "I'm really getting annoyed with this case. It feels as if we're being jerked around, and at this point, I don't know where else to look or who to torture."

"So we do things the hard way."

"Which is?" she asked, looking up at him.

"Keep our eyes open, and when trouble hits, fight back fast, hard, and dirty. You in, witch?"

Evangeline's lips tilted into a smile. "You know, sometimes I really admire the way you think. I'm definitely in. We'll make them sorry they ever decided to mess with Wicked Incorporated and her big pussycat."

He pretended affront and said, "Hey, I'm more than just a handsome sidekick," which quickly turned into an, "Aah, yes, whatever you say, just don't stop," as she fought his sudden tickle attack with her tongue and hands in sensitive places.

At the moment of her climax, she happened to peer up at him and lost herself in the heated gaze of his golden glowing eyes. She couldn't help the thought that ran through her mind as he came with a final, hard thrust. *Big, powerful, and ...mine.*

24

Ryker woke to a raging hard-on caused by one wicked witch who'd positioned herself between his legs.

"Have a nice nap?" she purred, wrapping her hands around his thick shaft. Her bright green eyes regarded him mischievously as she poised her lips above his mushroomed head.

Now there's something I wouldn't mind seeing every morning. He lost all coherent thought when she swirled her tongue around the tip of his cock, licking it lavishly like the yummiest of ice cream cones.

"I was thinking about the job," she said, stopping her delicious ministrations. "And I think I've come up with a plan."

"Sure." Without even hearing it, Ryker was prepared to agree, anything to get her back on track and continuing what she'd started with her mouth.

Her lips widened in a smile. "Aren't you the least bit curious about my plan?"

"*Heksen,* you've got my cock in your hand and your

mouth is an inch away. The only thing I'm curious about right now is how deep you can take me."

She eyed his length as if calculating, an up close perusal that made a drop of cum pearl at the tip of his shaft. Her tongue darted out and lapped it up, and Ryker couldn't help groaning.

"So anyway, I thought since we have no idea what to expect, we should try a bait and switch."

Ryker peered at her with hooded eyes. "Witch, I told you we'll do whatever you want. Just suck me."

"Like this?"

Ryker let out a shout and he dug his fingers into the sheets when she enveloped him in—completely. Her lips slid down, down, down the length of his shaft, unhesitating. She didn't stop until she touched the skin at the base. Her throat convulsed around his cock, so deep had she taken him, a hot, tight, and wet feeling that had him trembling in his attempt not to cum.

Slowly, her lips slid back up until, with a pop, she pulled her mouth off his cock. "Okay, now that your curiosity about my deep-throating abilities has been assuaged, let me tell you the rest of my plan."

Too aroused and stunned to speak, he listened as she outlined her plan. Brilliant, yet possibly dangerous, he had to admit it would probably give them their best shot.

"I don't like the fact you're placing yourself in danger," he growled.

She replied with a hard suck on his swollen head, which made his eyes roll back in his head. *Holy fuck, she's good.*

Coming up for air, she said, "I'll be fine. Besides, my big, bad kitty won't let anything happen to me."

His beast roared in agreement, and Ryker silently echoed. *No one will hurt my witch or I'll fucking kill them.*

"Now, we only have a little bit of time before I've got to get ready to go, so lie back and get ready to scream my name."

Ryker's hips bucked as her lips covered him again, the wet tightness of her mouth so erotic around his throbbing rod. She worked him fast. She sucked him hard. Ryker's head thrashed from side to side and his fingers dug into the mattress, tearing the sheet in his pleasure.

"I'm gonna cum," he managed to gasp, hoping she would stop so he could sink into her velvety softness, but instead, she gripped him more tightly, her sucking action never pausing.

He opened his eyes and looked down at her. He found her watching him, the wildness and arousal he could see in her eyes pushing him over the edge. Like a volcano, he shot his load, and she took it, every last drop. Then she swallowed, which blew Ryker away.

I am never *letting her go.*

* * *

THE SMOKING LOOK in Ryker's eyes when he came made Evangeline cream hard. She swallowed the hot juice that belonged to him uniquely.

I wish this could last forever. I've never felt like this about a man before.

With a smile and a lick of her lips, she went to get off the bed, but found herself flat on her back instead with a heavy body crushing hers.

"Hold onto the headboard," he growled.

Evangeline thought about arguing that she needed to shower and get ready, but the wild glow in his eyes promised pleasure, and her body needed release. Craved it.

She wrapped her fingers around the bars of her headboard. Ryker gave her a wicked smile before kneeling between her legs and spreading them wide.

"Sooo sweet," he whispered. Then he lifted her up and feasted on her.

He started out by nibbling her soft inner thighs, light, butterfly caresses that had her quickly panting, but unable to squirm in his firm grasp. The feel of his warm breath across her sensitive lower lips made her gasp.

"Ryker, please." She pleaded with him, too aroused to wait.

"Is *this* what you want?" he asked. His hot mouth opened wide and he took her, his tongue spreading her lips and lapping at the moistness within.

"Yes," she screamed, her fingers turning white where she gripped the bars tight.

He tortured her, his agile tongue licking her and flicking her clit. He alternated with sucking her and stabbing his tongue inside her, driving her wild with his mouth.

Evangeline's head thrashed from side to side, and she couldn't stop moaning, so close to the edge did he bring her.

"Come for me, *heksen*," he whispered against her sex before plunging three fingers inside, unerringly finding her g-spot and rubbing it. When he applied his tongue to her clit again while pumping her with his fingers, she lost it.

Pelvic muscles clenching, she came screaming as wave after wave of bliss crashed through her. And still he tortured her. His tongue flicked faster on her clit and his fingers kept rubbing her. Barely finished with her first orgasm, she went over the edge again, the ecstasy so overwhelming she blacked out for a moment.

Finally, he let her go. Laying himself alongside her, he cradled her in his arms, his lips lightly brushing her temple with kisses.

"*That's* just a teaser," he whispered to her. "Once the wedding is done and the plan executed successfully, I'm going to make love to you and make you cum so many times, you literally won't be able to walk."

Evangeline shuddered in his arms, which he tightened around her in a warm embrace she never wanted to leave.

Fuck me. She didn't know when it happened or how. But she could deny it no longer.

I think I fell in love. Nah. It was probably just the after glow from sex. Wicked witches did not love big, dumb cats. Even if they purred.

25

THE EIGHT HOUR DIFFERENCE BETWEEN THE UNITED STATES and St. Petersburg meant they had to be showered and ready to go by four AM. They'd used the few hours they had left before to hash out the details of Evangeline's plan and to meet with Rumpelstiltskin to ensure he was on board.

With a hard kiss, Ryker admonished her to be careful, a warning that had her eyes widen in surprise then soften in a look he'd rarely seen. It shocked him to realize that something so minor as showing he cared about her would make her react. If only she knew how much she meant to him. For a moment, he almost blurted it out loud, however, surrounded by chattering strangers, on the verge of completing their mission was hardly the time to declare his love. He kept silent, but kissed her again even though she hissed at him to behave.

Her cheeks blooming with color and her lipstick askew, she left with the first group through the portal that would take them halfway across the world in the space of a few seconds.

Fuck did he hate magic and anything to do with Hell. He especially distrusted the demons provided by Satan to open the portals for the guests to arrive quickly and comfortably, but he had to admit it beat a stupidly long plane trip and having to put up with TSA thugs. But even more than his dislike of the wormhole type travel, he hated having Evangeline leave ahead of him.

His beast paced, anxious at the fact its mate—*our mate*—was so far from them. Knowing she could take care of herself didn't alleviate his unease; rather, it amplified it, because he knew how much trouble she could cause. An endearing quality most of the time, but only so long as he could be on hand to help her out if trouble arose.

Finally, his turn arrived, and joining the group of wedding guests that included Rumpelstiltskin and Tina, they went through the portal, the non-human magic working even for shifters.

Seconds later, emerging from the portal, Ryker blinked in the bright sunlight and gazed in begrudging admiration at the Catherine palace where the wedding would soon take place. Ostentatious, but definitely impressive. Having pulled the first round of nanny duty because, as his witch put it, he didn't need to do anything to make himself look pretty, he followed a few paces behind Rumpelstiltskin and his little girl.

Ryker still couldn't believe he was attending the wedding of the anti-Christ, not to mention said man would be marrying Evangeline's sister. *What kind of family am I getting into?* It would sure make for interesting family get-togethers.

Speaking of family, his mother, when he'd returned to his house for toiletries and his suit, seemed resigned to his new married state. As a matter of fact, she'd seemed to have embraced it, gleefully making plans to introduce her new daughter-in-law at the next full moon.

When Ryker questioned the wisdom of such an act, she'd grinned, in quite an evil fashion, and said, "The more I think of it, the more I think I'll like our new alignment with the witch. Do you know that your father's security company has already gotten calls from the Russian coven asking them to do some protective detail?"

Word sure traveled fast. Or at least his mother's gossip did. But at least his dad was now talking to him again. A shame. He'd rather enjoyed the silence.

* * *

INSIDE THE PALACE, ensconced in a room with too many women, Evangeline had to restrain herself from running even though her sister seemed determined to drive her to it.

"I look fat, don't I?" Isobel said, twirling to look at her ass in the mirror.

"Your scrawny butt is still as skinny as the rest of you," reassured Evangeline. "Would you untangle your knickers from the knot you've put them in?"

"Are you implying I'm nervous?"

"Duh."

"Don't duh me. I was just remarking that this dress is all wrong. I can't go out in public like this."

"Stop freaking out. You're just anxious."

"Maybe a little. How do I know I'm making the right choice? I mean, look at who his father is. I'm not evil enough to be Satan's daughter-in-law. How will I ever fit in?"

"You love Christopher, don't you?"

"Of course I do," said Isobel, blinking. "He's everything I've ever wanted in a man."

"Then shut up about the dress. You love him. He loves you. Everything else will work out."

Isobel let out a big breath and straightened her shoulders. "You're right. It will. Hold on a second. Did I hear you right? Did you actually use the L-word?"

Evangeline shot her sister a dirty look.

"Holy fuck. You did. Interesting. So how are you and that hunky shifter of yours doing?" asked Isobel slyly, adjusting her neckline to deepen her cleavage.

"He's not mine," mumbled Evangeline. *Although, his beast did mark me as his. I just wish I knew how the* man *feels about me.*

"Oh, please. Anyone could tell the two of you are meant for each other."

"He's an animal."

"And? My soon-to-be husband is the son of the Devil. Big whoop."

"Big difference. I mean, do you really think Granddad would go for it? Or Mother?" Evangeline actually didn't care what her family thought, but she wanted Isobel off her back.

"Actually, Mother likes him."

"She *what?*" Evangeline just stared at her sister, dumbstruck.

"She had coffee with him when we were doing the

dress fittings and she's all for it. She just says it's a shame you can't make babies."

"I don't like babies, remember?" said Evangeline with a glower, not understanding why she felt a pang at the thought of never having a cute and sweet little boy that resembled Ryker with his vivid blue eyes.

And at that thought, Evangeline finally knew without a shadow of doubt. It wasn't just good sex. Or hatred. Or indigestion. *I love him.*

Sitting down hard, something of her shock must have registered in her face, because her sister rushed over and clasped her hands between hers. "What's wrong? You've got the oddest look on your face."

She spoke without thinking. "I love him."

"But that's wonderful," exclaimed Isobel.

Having said it aloud, she wanted to vomit. Evangeline's brow knotted in confusion. "I don't know if I'd call it that. Just saying it is nauseating me."

"Only because you don't know how he feels. Just ask him. You'll feel better."

A violent shake of her head was her answer to that. "Ask him? Are you nuts? Besides, I already know he doesn't love me back."

"Are you sure about that?"

Considering he had ample opportunity to declare it when he explained the whole mating thing? Yeah, she could definitely say he didn't. "We're just compatible in bed. Nothing more."

"I think you're wrong. Tell him you love him. Suck up pride, put on your big girl panties, and admit for once how you feel," said Isobel, patting her hand. "I think you might be surprised at his answer."

Admit my feelings? What if he rejects or mocks me? I can't even turn him into a frog. Nor did she think she had it in her to kill him at this point, now knowing how she felt about him.

There was a knock on the door and the wedding planner from Hell—literally—stuck her horned demon head around the jamb. "It's time, ladies. Let's get this show moving."

Clutching a bouquet of blood red roses, Evangeline wore a scowl as she started her walk down the aisle created in the ballroom between the sections of seats. Her grimace, though, faded when she saw him.

Ryker stood devastatingly tall and handsome with the other groomsmen. When their eyes met, his lips curled into a grin just for her. His blue eyes smoldered with appreciation and Evangeline couldn't help the brilliant smile that burst forth. What a shame they couldn't ditch this matrimonial circus and find a secluded closet somewhere, or even just a private corner.

Standing on the bride's side, she couldn't stop staring at Ryker, and even odder, he never took his eyes off her.

Mentally slapping herself, she reminded herself that they were still on a job, not to mention her sister was getting married. She flicked a look over at little Tina, who stood beside her, waiting her turn to sing, then at Isobel who stared up at her prince of Hell with so much joy it made Evangeline sick.

Oh fuck, I hope I don't wear the same vapid expression when I stare at Ryker.

Finally, the ceremony came to a close, and the presiding hooded figure said, "I now pronounce you man and wife. May you live forever, and a gruesome curse befall any who would rip you asunder."

Those words were the cue for Tina to step forward and do her thing. She might appear shy and frail, however, the voice that burst forth from her petite form would have made angels weep—if they dared show up at the wedding a step away from Hell. The child truly possessed a musical gift, and as she sang of love and commitment, Evangeline couldn't help peeking over at Ryker. Their gazes met and she shivered at the burning expression in his eyes.

A last lingering note by the youthful prodigy and the audience burst in thunderous applause. The ceremony over, people—and other beings not often seen on the mortal plane—began to mill. Evangeline and Ryker flanked Tina as they made their way behind the couple, stopping every few feet as congratulations echoed from all sides. Once they cleared the ceremonial room, they went off to the garden for photos while the rest of the guests enjoyed pre-dinner cocktails.

Personally, Evangeline would have skipped the whole photo session, however, her mother and sister had bullied her into agreeing to pose for a few. While Evangeline scowled at the camera, Ryker hovered around Tina and her father. As soon as she could, though, she escaped and met up with Ryker and her patron.

"Okay, time to do this. Come on," she said, leading the way, tossing her bouquet at a startled nymph.

They went as a group to the dining hall without mishap. Plates in hand, they browsed the varied foods set up on display as a buffet, a vast selection to tempt all kinds of palates—although Evangeline wondered who would want to eat the live frogs and worms.

Gazes watchful, senses on high alert, they ate their meal. Tina sat tucked between them while Ryker pretended to down copious amounts of alcohol. Around them, beings of all kind talked and laughed. The guests ranged from human looking to demonic, with other fairy tale creatures in between. Nobody wanted to miss out on the event of the century. But who planned to use the commotion as a guise to kidnap or harm the little girl in their care?

So far, no one stood out.

The longer they sat without anything happening, the more her impatience grew. Yet, at the same time, anticipation and its accompanying rush filled her as the time for the execution of their plan neared.

Dinner done, and the cutting of the cake accomplished, without bloodshed—how disappointing—the crowd flowed back into the ballroom for the dancing that would begin shortly. Evangeline thanked the fact her sister had vetoed speeches at her wedding, or else things might have gotten ugly considering the amount of alcohol being siphoned by the guests. While she dearly loved her grandfather, once he got a few glasses of vodka into him, he could get quite colorful, and easily riled.

The band from Hell—Satan's Rockers—got the party going, and after Isobel, beaming up at her new husband, got her first dance, other people hit the dance floor. That was their signal. Evangeline threw a sideways glance at Ryker and nodded her head.

With a smile meant to look drunken, but which she

personally found rakish, Ryker grabbed her ass and squeezed. Evangeline let out a shriek and slapped him.

"You dirty shifter. Keep your fucking hands to yourself."

"Admit it. You want me. I've seen you eyeing me."

"Because I wondered who let the dirty animal in."

"Dirty? I'll show you dirty." He grabbed his crotch, squeezed, and leered. She almost laughed.

"You are a pig!"

"And you're an uptight witch," he taunted back. "I've got something to fix that. Drop to your knees and I'll give you the cure for free."

"That's it," she exclaimed, whirling to Rumpelstiltskin. "I will not work with this asshole any longer. I quit." Turning on her heel, she stalked from the room and, in order to make it believable, went through a waiting portal away from the wedding.

Now came the sneaky, fun part.

26

Abandoned by his partner, all part of the plan, Ryker followed Tina to the ladies room and after taking a quick peek inside, let her in alone. He stood outside with his arms folded over his chest, waiting.

Several minutes later, Tina came skipping back out.

"Ready, witch?" he murmured in a low tone.

"Let's nab some bad guys," Evangeline replied, her voice high pitched like a young girl's.

Ryker hoped her plan worked. At least no matter what happened, Tina would be safe. Spirited away secretly to a place only Rumpelstiltskin knew of, Tina would spend the rest of the evening playing video games and watching television under heavy guard while his witch, under the cover of a glamor, took Tina's place and made herself the target.

Escorting her back to the ballroom, he saw Rumpelstiltskin look over at them and he inclined his head slightly to indicate the plan was in motion.

Now he needed to find a believable distraction so that someone could attempt to nab the fake Tina.

Turned out he didn't need to look far because the diversion found him.

"There you are," said a soft voice belonging to none other than his ex-fiancée, Vivian.

"Vivian," he said, turning to face her.

Clad in a shimmering teal gown that set off the platinum of her hair nicely, he found his short-lived fiancée beautiful; however, she stirred nothing in him, not even hatred.

"Hello, Ryker," she said, smiling at him tremulously.

Ryker wanted to walk away, because he really had nothing to say to the woman, but from the corner of his eye, he could see his disguised witch still weaving through the crowd. No one had made a move on her yet.

"Why are you here?" he asked suddenly. "You aren't acquainted with either the bride or the groom."

"What do you mean why? You invited me. I have to say I was surprised given what happened between us. But I've had time to think and mother—"

Ryker stopped listening. *Fuck, Vivian's a plant to distract me.* His eyes searched the crowded room and just in time. He caught a glimpse of Tina, holding her mother, Heidi's, hand and leaving the ballroom.

Sprinting through the crowd, he began unbuttoning his shirt, jostling revelers. *Fuck this.* With a roar, his beast burst through his tux and landed with a soft thud on the marbled floor. Given the gathering of magical and supernatural beings, no one even batted an eye as he moved through them quickly in his panther form.

Slipping through the door his disguised witch had

exited with Heidi, he peered around. A flash of color caught his eye. Slinking through the darkness, he crept up and heard voices.

"I brought her like you asked, darling," said Heidi.

Peering through the bushes that hid his quarry, Ryker coiled his hind legs, ready to spring.

A stranger smiled coldly at Heidi. "There's a good girl. Now go back to the ballroom and forget any of this happened." With a wave of his hands, the male used magic on Tina's mother who, with a vacuous smile, headed back the way she'd come.

Shit, a wizard.

"As for you, little girl, we're going to go on a little trip."

Tina's little girl shape disappeared and Evangeline, looking like a delicious pink bonbon in her bridesmaid's dress, shook her head at the wizard. "I don't think so, asshole."

"Who the hell are you?" snapped the wizard.

"Your worst nightmare."

Ozone permeated the air, the smell distinctive, as was the crackling energy as his witch drew magic into herself. The static electricity of it made her hair flutter, and her eyes turned black.

However, when she released her magic against Heidi's mysterious friend, nothing happened, to him at least. However, the magical backlash knocked Evangeline back. She flew through the air and hit the trunk of a tree with a hard thump. Her limp body slumped to the ground in a frothy heap of lace and satin.

The bastard laughed and held up an amulet. "Sorry, witch, but with this special artifact I found in Merlin's tomb, I am immune against magical attack."

But not big kitty ones.

With a snarl of rage, Ryker pounced, all four claws out and fangs just aching for a target.

* * *

EVANGELINE SHOOK HER HEAD, trying to clear it. *Fucker had a magical shield.* And like a rookie out of magic school, she tossed a spell right at it. Dumb. Dumb. Dumb. Her grandfather would have smacked her a second time if he'd caught her acting so cocky with an unknown sorcerer.

Sitting up, she shook off her daze in time to see Ryker, sporting his black panther form, come sailing out of nowhere to land on the wizard.

"Get him, kitty." She whispered the words, her bloodthirsty nature not averse to seeing the man who'd bested her torn to shreds. As it turned out, the wizard—who was really starting to piss her off—had more than one trick up his sleeve. With nary a trace of magic, the wizard suddenly became a striped white tiger, and since touching Ryker didn't dispel the illusion, the only conclusion she could come to was the stranger was both wizard and shifter. *I'll be damned. What happened to the species not being able to mix?*

Snarling and slashing, the two massive beasts rolled through the bushes onto the dimly lit terrace, their claws raking bloody grooves.

Evangeline could only watch helplessly and it roused her anger to a boiling pitch.

Ryker's getting hurt. I need to stop this, but how? I can't use my magic on them.

At least not while he's wearing that amulet.

"Ryker, pull off his amulet."

Teeth suddenly clamping around the dangling ornament, Ryker tore it from the wizard's feline neck. But in doing so, he left himself open and the white tiger who, with a roar of rage, scored his claws down Ryker's side, opening several deep, bleeding lacerations. Then the bastard turned to snarl at her. But she didn't care about the threat to herself, not when her lover lay bleeding on the ground.

"Son of a bitch!" Evangeline screamed. "How dare you fucking hurt him!"

Sucking into herself an immense amount of power, enough it burned along her nerves, haloed her hair, and made her skin fairly steam she held so much, she flung it all at the white tiger, only belatedly realizing that being part-shifter, the magic might not work.

She needn't have feared. Apparently, only a full shifter could dispel a witch's magic. With wide eyes and a horrified scream, the wizard-shifter hybrid turned into a grease spot on the terrace.

Wild clapping erupted and Evangeline looked over to see a crowd had gathered to watch the fight.

Ignoring them, Evangeline ran over to the panther who lay on the ground, chest heaving, blood seeping. As she approached, he reverted back to his naked, human male body.

Dropping to her knees beside him, she could see the crimson fluid streaking his skin.

"Ryker," she cried. "Don't you dare die, you big, dumb cat. You can't die."

"A kiss," he gasped.

Immediately, she ducked down, and finding his lips,

sealed hers to his. *He's dying, oh fuck. Why did this have to happen?* It figured that just when she found a man she could love, he would get himself killed. She couldn't stop the tears from forming, and one dripped onto his face. "Oh, Ryker."

His lips continued to devour hers hungrily and he murmured against them, "My sweet *heksen*, you didn't really think a puny jerk like that could kill me, did you?"

Evangeline rocked back on her heels and glared at him with sudden suspicion. "I saw your injuries. He practically ripped your guts out."

"And I am a shifter with excellent recuperative powers." Ryker swiped at the drying blood and showed her the already closing wounds. He also showed off his very large erection, which garnered quite the collection of gasps and titters from the watching crowd.

Cheeks burning, Evangeline got up. "I'll go find you some clothes."

And perhaps strike some women blind while I'm at it, she thought, eyeing the chattering gaggle who wouldn't stop pointing and staring at her naked man.

"Anyone who wants to live, leave now," she snarled, not caring if she appeared jealous. *He's mine.*

However, her words had the desired effect and the crowd moved back indoors.

Now to find some clothes so she could dress Ryker long enough to get him somewhere where she could undress him and fuck him for scaring her. Then she'd screw him again for coming to her rescue. Then...

Hmm, considering what she planned to do, she'd better grab some food as well to keep them energized.

27

Ryker almost laughed when his witch made the gawkers scatter. At least she seemed uninjured. The rage he'd felt when that wizard had hurt her...well, it was a good thing she'd turned him into a grease spot because his plans for the bastard involved a lot more blood and screaming, which might not have gone over well considering this was a wedding.

Even better, with the bad guy out of the way and the job done, it meant he could now indulge in his fantasy of peeling her out of the girly dress and making her scream in an entirely erotic fashion. He'd not missed her cry of rage when he'd gotten hurt. *I do believe my witch cares for me.* Something he planned to make her admit to later on when he got her alone and naked. The things he planned to do to her...

Standing up, uncaring of his nudity—*if you've got it, flaunt it*—he waited for her to return, his face craned up at the half moon.

"Oh, Ryker, that was so brave," gushed Vivian from behind him.

For fuck's sake. Not now. Ryker whirled and saw his ex-fiancée, eyes aglow with admiration, a look Ryker had never seen before on her face, and one that rendered her quite pretty. However, she didn't even come close to comparing with his witch, whom he craned around looking for. *I'd better get rid of Vivian before she gets back.* Somehow, he didn't think Evangeline would take the time to listen to excuses. Or show mercy.

"Listen Viv—"

The body that plastered itself to him and kissed him took him by surprise. Incredulous, he peered down at Vivian. She had her eyes closed and was pressing herself passionately against him. Unfortunately for her, it left him cold.

However, he knew someone who would be more than hot if she saw this pathetic attempt.

When he heard the snarled, "Bitch, get your hands off my man," he realized it was already too late and prepared to enjoy the fireworks.

Vivian pulled back with a smirk. "You must be the witch he's been sleeping with. Well, you can just go find yourself a new boy toy. The engagement is back on, right, darling?"

Ryker raised his hands and shook his head at Vivian. "Like fuck. I've found my mate, and if I were you, I'd run because she is *not* happy you touched me."

Evangeline graced him with a smile that made him harder than a rock, and then with a snarl, she turned to Vivian, who stupidly stood her ground.

"Listen up and listen good, you little fucking bitch.

Ryker is mine, as in do not touch, look, or think of him, *mine.*"

Was it wrong that he enjoyed the way she stated her possession of him?

"But you're a witch. You can't be a couple," said Vivian stubbornly.

"You know what? Screw being diplomatic, you stupid cow." Evangeline drew back her fist and cold cocked Vivian, dropping her hard. "You're lucky I'm in such a good mood, or I'd be gutting you right now." Eyes dark with anger and her skin practically sparking, Evangeline glanced at him, as if daring him to say something.

Damn but jealousy looked hot on her. Ryker's heart filled with love for his feisty, evil witch. *And I am not waiting a second longer to tell her.*

28

"You really are evil, aren't you?" Ryker said, his words a cruel reminder of what so many others had said to her. Of course, she hadn't cared what they thought. *But I care what Ryker thinks.*

Evangeline hung her head in response, ashamed at the tears that pricked her eyes. Calloused fingers gripped her chin and tilted her face back up.

"What the hell are you crying for?" he asked, aghast. "I was just stating the obvious."

"I'm sorry, but I refuse to be some perfect fucking Barbie doll. I can't help myself. Evil runs in my genes."

"Why the hell would I want a dumb, cookie cutter doll when I can have you?"

"But I'm not nice," she replied dumbly.

"Screw a nice girl. I want a wicked witch. Besides, I happen to like watching you at work."

Evangeline suddenly couldn't breathe, and she obviously couldn't hear because it had sounded like he'd said he wanted her.

"Ah, my sweet *heksen*, don't tell me you haven't figured it out yet. I thought you were supposed to be the smart one."

"Spell it out for me," she asked, wanting him to say it.

"I love you. I love every evil inch of you. And now that I've proven I'm braver and said it first, what about you?"

"I love you too, you big, stupid beast."

His thick arms crushed her ribs as he swung her around enthusiastically and let out a roar of excitement.

"So when do you want to officially tie the knot?"

"I thought we were mated?"

"In the eyes of shifters, but I imagine your mother would appreciate something more traditional."

"Is this your obtuse way of asking me to marry you?"

"Oh, please, if I got on my knee, you'd just hurt me. What do you say? Wanna get hitched? White dress, priest, the whole nine yards?"

Evangeline's eyes almost bugged out of her head. "Eew! What is wrong with you?"

Howling with laughter, Ryker swung her round again. "Just kidding."

"Listen, can't we just live in sin for a while? I'm really not keen on the idea of going through all that," she said, jerking her head at the castle where the sounds of revelry floated out to them on the terrace.

"Ooh, more sinning," he said with a leer. "Count me in."

"Here, put these on before I have to hurt someone else," she said, handing him the clothes she'd picked up from their hidden emergency stash. Although, personally, she preferred him naked. First things first, though, they needed to let Rumpelstiltskin know they'd succeeded in taking care of the villain just in case he hadn't heard. Afterwards, she planned to claim every inch of her lover's luscious body.

As soon as they walked in the door, Rumpelstiltskin cornered them, a grin creasing his ugly mug. "An excellent job once again by Wicked Incorporated. I've had your fee deposited already. Plus, at the requests of your respective mothers, who informed me of your mated status, I've thrown in a bonus. Congratulations, I've granted you the ability to reproduce with each other."

Evangeline went still as Rumpelstiltskin's words penetrated. "You. Did. What?" she said, using a full lungful of air for each word and taking a menacing step forward.

Rumpelstiltskin chuckled nervously. "Now, Evangeline, trust me. You'll thank me for this later."

"You're assuming you're going to survive the next five minutes."

At her side, Ryker started laughing deep guffaws. In between his mirth, he said, "Dude, if I were you, I'd run, 'cause I am not stupid enough to try and stop her."

With an undignified squeak, the ugly male turned and fled, but not quick enough to escape Evangeline's revenge. Sucking in an obscene amount of magic, she saw with her magically enhanced eyes the glamor her former employer hid under and she ripped it away.

Then she laughed, for instead of seeing Rumpelstiltskin's usual gnarly mug, his real form appeared: a six-foot-something blond Adonis. His face? A chiseled work of perfection, while his muscles rippled through the tattered clothing he'd torn in his sudden growth spurt.

Squeals erupted from a band of nymphs in the corner. "Master, you've returned to pleasure us!" Like an ocean of lemurs, they, and others of the female persuasion, came in a rippling wave of hair and pastel colors.

Rumpelstiltskin turned his transformed face to her, a look of horror etched on it. "Now that was just evil."

Evangeline just crossed her arms over her chest. "Yes, yes it was. Next time you meddle in someone's life, ask first. Now I'd suggest you run; it will be twenty four hours before you can put your ugly glamor back on."

Poor Rumpelstiltskin, he tried to run, but his new long stride was no match for the determined women who mobbed him. Off they carted him despite his screams to leave him alone.

Ryker's strong arms wrapped around her, and his breath tickled her ear when he said, "Dammit, *heksen*, you are so wickedly hot. Let's go practice making a baby."

Her foot slamming his instep didn't stop him from throwing her over his shoulder and striding through a crowd that didn't even look twice—after all, at the antichrist's wedding, some indiscretions were expected as par for the course.

29

In a palace this size, Ryker didn't find it hard to locate an empty room with a bed. He threw her onto the soft mattress. While he locked the door, Evangeline stripped out of her clothes, a fact that made his eyes glow golden with appreciation when he turned around.

Finally naked, she smiled and beckoned to him. He stripped out of his shirt and pants first, his jutting erection bobbing eagerly at her as he strode to the bed.

Laying his body on top of hers, she winced. He rolled off her instantly.

"You're hurt? Where?" His hands smoothed over skin and not finding anything on her front, he flipped her to her stomach and she heard him suck in a breath.

"It's just a bruise," she said.

"You're injured," Ryker growled.

"So kiss it better," she said, looking back at him over her shoulder.

He did, his lips caressing her bruised skin and then moving down her back to the crevice of her ass. He spread her cheeks and thighs, his calloused fingers finding her wet and ready for him.

"Get on your hands and knees. I can't wait. I need you now."

Evangeline quickly obeyed, her need for him just as urgent. The head of his cock speared her, its hard length sliding in and filling her up. He grabbed her waist and began pumping her, and Evangeline gasped.

"Don't." Thrust. "You." Pound. "Ever." Quicker. "Scare me like that again," he finally said as he pistoned his hips.

"Same to you," she panted.

He found her clit with wet fingers and rubbed it until the stimulation was enough to make her scream and send her over the edge. But Ryker wasn't yet done with her. He grabbed a handful of her hair and she eagerly arched back. "I mean it, witch. You are mine. All mine. And just so you know, this time, I know exactly what I'm doing. I choose you as my mate, every wicked inch of you. For now and always." He leaned forward, still thrusting, and his sharp teeth found the soft flesh of her nape and bit down, marking her a second time.

Oh, the ecstasy. With a shuddering cry, she gushed and convulsed in the throes of a major orgasm. Wave after wave of bliss crashed through her body and her vaginal muscles squeezed him tightly. With a final deep lunge and a bellow, he came inside her.

They collapsed on the bed, a heaving mess of naked flesh. She'd never been happier. He rolled to the side and dragged her atop him.

"I love you," he said, his chest rumbling under her cheek.

"I love you too." She couldn't believe how easily the words rolled off her tongue and how right they felt.

"Now, before I wash every inch of you with my tongue, I've got to ask, because since our fake fight, people have bombarded me with rumors. Which of them are true?"

"All of them, of course."

He tilted her chin up so he could look her in the face and Evangeline grinned, which was so unlike her, but dammit, being around him made her...happy.

"So you did turn Derek into a doormat?" he asked.

"Rat, actually. Jerk dumped me for being too evil." What a pity the spell only lasted twenty-four hours.

"Derek was an idiot. You're just confident, nothing wrong with that. What about the guy you glued to the hood of a police cruiser, naked?"

"Beating up hookers."

"Grease puddle later identified as Gary Whitecloak?"

"Magical rapist." Evangeline had set herself up as bait one night, and the look on his face before she turned him into a melted popsicle—priceless.

"I hate to break it to you," Ryker said after a few more queries about her reputation. "But you're not evil."

"What are you talking about?" Evangeline huffed, leaning up on his chest. "I am ruthless and take no shit."

"Yeah, but from what you've told me, everyone's deserved it. I mean, do you go out and kill innocents?"

"Of course not," she said, frowning.

"What if they called you a bad name?"

"I have more control than that," she said, rolling her eyes. "Although, I might make them grovel a bit."

"See, you're actually not all that wicked."

She squirmed up and straddled him. "Take that back. I am the wickedest."

"In the bedroom maybe."

"If you tell anyone otherwise, I'll masturbate and make you watch with no touching."

His eyes widened in horror. "I take it back. You are the wickedest witch ever. And even better, you're all mine."

His words made Evangeline glow and feel all warm and mushy inside. They also made her horny. Good thing he had a lot of stamina, something she made good use of that night, numerous times.

EPILOGUE

Ryker's arm curled tight around Evangeline's frame, and he smiled contentedly from their perch on the roof of the library. Halloween night had arrived with clear skies and a rare full moon. Dusk had already fallen and children were out in costumed hordes, their cheerful voices floating up into the night sky.

"Ready?" he asked, giving her a squeeze.

"Totally," Evangeline said with a grin. Moving away from Ryker, she put her glamor into place, a hideous crone of a witch replete with a wart and strawlike black hair.

Ryker shuddered. "That is absolutely hideous."

With a grin that revealed yellowed buckteeth, she cackled. "Your turn."

Ryker's body rippled and out sprang his black panther. With gloves on, lest he disrupt her magic, she gave her beast a quick scratch that had him purring, then she pulled out the harness they'd had specially made and strapped the baby saddle to Ryker's transformed back. She plopped their daughter—Mortika—into the customized seat.

Impending motherhood had initially been a cruel shock—she'd gone on a rampage that had done wonders for her already evil reputation and brought in a flood of jobs for Wicked Incorporated. Lucky for the mortals, she'd not done much permanent damage during her pregnancy. They *really* hadn't been kidding about those mood swings.

Once she'd gotten over the anger and morning sickness—something that had made Rumpelstiltskin leave town in terror—the birth of her daughter had turned into a surprisingly fulfilling experience. There was nothing like seeing one's own flesh and blood performing her first evil deed—wiggling chubby little fingers to steal another child's lollipop. And she became her father's pride and joy when she turned into a frisky, sharp-clawed kitten.

Now, to Evangeline's delight, she was about to introduce her daughter to a yearly tradition—ruining Halloween.

"Remember, sweetie," Evangeline said to her blue-eyed vixen who clapped her chubby hands in glee. "The important thing is to have fun at the expense of others."

Watching with a smile as Ryker bounded among the costumed children, their daughter giggling away, Evangeline felt her heart swell. She might still be the Wickedest Witch, but dammit, against all odds, she'd found true love, and she'd do *anything*—even kill—to keep it.

THE END - BUT IF YOU'RE CURIOUS ABOUT ISOBEL AND CHRISTOPHER, THEN CHECK OUT LAZY SON.

- **For more warped stories see** <u>EveLanglais.com</u>
- **Newsletter:** <u>Sign Up Here</u>

www.ingramcontent.com/pod-product-compliance
Lightning Source LLC
LaVergne TN
LVHW041634060526
838200LV00040B/1564